THE SECRET BATTLE OF
EVAN PAO

Also by Wendy Wan-Long Shang

The Great Wall of Lucy Wu

The Way Home Looks Now

with Madelyn Rosenberg

This Is Just a Test

Not Your All-American Girl

THE SECRET BATTLE OF
EVAN PAO

WENDY WAN-LONG SHANG

SCHOLASTIC PRESS /NEW YORK

Library of Congress Cataloging-in-Publication Data available

ISBN 978-1-338-67885-7

10 9 8 7 6 5 4 3 2 1   22 23 24 25 26

Printed in Italy   183
First edition, May 2022

Book design by Keirsten Geise

TO MY FAMILY, WITH LOVE

CHAPTER ONE

EVAN

When they reached Virginia, their tenth and final state, Evan took out the three Jolly Ranchers he'd been carefully saving since Indiana and passed them out. Sour apple for Mom and himself; cherry for Celeste.

"To celebrate making it to Virginia," he announced. It'd been hard to save the last bit of candy, but it was worth it. They'd been in the car so long that any little new thing felt like relief. He popped the candy into his mouth, letting the sweetness spread over his tongue.

"'We're not in Kansas anymore,'" quipped Celeste as she unwrapped the candy.

"Technically speaking, we never went through Kansas," said Evan. "We did, however, go through Nevada, Utah, Wyoming,

Nebraska, Iowa, Illinois, Indiana . . ." Evan had designated himself the navigator for the trip. He liked knowing where they were, what was coming. He traced his fingers along the route.

"It's a quote from *The Wizard of Oz*," said Celeste. "The moment when Dorothy goes outside after a tornado and discovers Oz. The point is, she's not home. Kansas is beside the point." She pulled on a strand of hair, already bored by her own explanation.

Evan tried to switch to sitting cross-legged, which necessitated moving an old box of french fries and not spilling his water. For a while, it felt like the car was a spaceship and they were adventurers making their way across the country, watching the landscape change shape and color. Spring looked different everywhere, but Evan had to admit that spring in Virginia was the prettiest, with green grass and trees blooming with pink and white flowers. When they first started, Mom had all sorts of ambitious plans, like keeping a cooler filled with healthy snacks and practicing Chinese. But after six days of nonstop driving, the car felt more like a trash can at a fast-food restaurant and the only new Chinese phrase Evan was certain he'd learned was *zhīshì hànbǎo*, "cheeseburger."

"Old movies are weird," said Evan. The candy clacked around his mouth as he talked. He didn't really think that. He just wanted Celeste to put her phone down and talk to him.

"It's a classic," said Celeste. "Everyone should see it. There are so many references to it. The Wicked Witch. The Tin Man without a heart." Being three years older, Celeste had a lot of opinions on things *everyone* should know, or do, or think.

"It's not as important as *Star Wars*, though," argued Evan. "The Force, Darth Vader. Jedi."

During the course of the trip, they had argued over the best Marvel movie, the tastiest pasta shape, the right way to tie a shoe, and whether cats were smarter than dogs. Mom sighed. "Almost there, guys." It was her way of saying, don't start fighting. "We're almost at the end."

It's almost the beginning, too, Evan thought. He wasn't sure if he felt happy or nervous about that. He pressed his face against the window. Tree. House. Tree. House. Roadside stand. They passed a house with a girl throwing a Frisbee to a black-and-white dog. "At least Dorothy had a dog," he said.

Mom sighed. "You know that things have just been too unsettled to get a dog." Evan disagreed. It was always a good time

3

to get a dog. Maybe you needed a dog the most when things were down.

"You mean, Dad taking off and us moving all the way across the country to a town where we know exactly one person? That kind of unsettled?" said Celeste. "Or did you mean something else?"

"That would be it," said Mom quietly. From the back seat, Evan watched his mom's shoulders hunch over. He nudged Celeste and tilted his head toward Mom.

"Sorry," said Celeste. They had an unspoken agreement not to talk about Dad, but sometimes it just popped up, like a ball being held underwater.

"We'll be okay," said Evan. "We'll un-unsettle." He paused. "And then we'll get a dog."

"Hope springs eternal for Evan," said Mom. She shifted in her seat, trying to find a way to be comfortable.

"At least when it comes to dogs," said Evan.

They stopped at a gas station. Mom said it should be the last fill-up they needed. A man came out of the store and cocked his head sideways at them, watching them stumble out of the car to stretch and get the feeling of the earth beneath them again.

4

"You folks lost?" he asked. There wasn't any particular concern in his voice. It was more like amusement, Evan thought.

"We're fine," said Mom. "Just need some gas." She unhooked the nozzle and stuck it into the car.

The man took a couple steps toward them. "I heard your tires when you came in," said the man. "Might be something wrong with your alignment. You oughta get 'em checked out." He jerked his head toward the garage. "I gotta free bay. I could run your car up on the rack for you."

Mom hesitated. Dad usually took care of car maintenance. Had taken care of car maintenance. "If your car's out of alignment and you keep driving, you're going to get uneven wear on the tire, maybe damage the CV joints . . ." said the man.

Mom threw Evan a look. Evan didn't know about cars, but Mom's question was different. Evan shook his head, barely. *No. Don't trust him.*

"We'll have our mechanic take a look," said Mom. "But thank you for pointing that out." She smiled. It wasn't Mom's real smile, but the man didn't know that.

The man sighed, as if they had disappointed him. "Suit yourself. That's a nice car." It was a nice car, a Mercedes-Benz SUV. It was one of the last vestiges of their old life.

Mom paid for the gas and they got back in the car. "What was that about?" said Celeste. She kept her voice low, even though the man could not hear them. "Why was he saying there's something wrong with the car? You had it checked out before we left California."

"He probably saw the out-of-town plates, figured he might make a quick buck," said Mom. "Right, Evan?"

"He didn't feel right," said Evan. That's all he knew, usually all he ever knew. The reasons and the motivations, that was beyond his perception.

"Then why were you so nice to him?" asked Celeste. "If Evan said he was lying?"

Mom flipped the turn signal, changed lanes. "We're never going to see him again. Why anger him? Put your head down and don't cause trouble."

Evan had a sense for lies. When he was younger, he didn't know what it was. He had started feeling sick after baseball games. Mom and Dad had thought it was the stress of pitching but it was more than that.

It was the coach, Mr. Nelson, saying that he didn't care

if they won or lost, clapping his hands and cheering on the team, but Evan could see that he really did care. His jaw became tight when the team started to fall behind, and he stopped talking so much. When they won, Mr. Nelson liked hanging around, soaking up the win, but when they lost, he jumped in his car and left as soon as possible. Once, he left an equipment bag behind because he was in such a hurry.

During the playoffs, right before they ran out of the dugout, Mr. Nelson gripped Evan by the shoulder and told Evan that he was a good pitcher, and that he'd be proud of Evan no matter what happened. Just go out there and do your best.

The words were like a punch to the head. Evan felt dizzy, as if he were seeing double. In one frame, the coach was smiling and supportive, *You're a great pitcher! Just do your best!* In the other frame, the coach was tense and unhappy, whispering, *Just strike these guys out, okay? I really want to win.* The coach wasn't really saying those words, but Evan could hear the words of what the coach really wanted, slithering underneath the words he was saying out loud. There were two movies, playing side by side, but he could not get them to come into one coherent image.

Evan promptly ran out to the mound and threw up.

7

"You should have told us you weren't feeling well," Mom said on the way home. Evan was in the back seat, holding an empty jumbo soda cup, in case he felt sick again. Evan ended up not pitching, but he stayed in the dugout, watching.

"It came on all of the sudden," said Evan sadly. The coaches put sand over the throw-up, but the damage was done. Evan's team lost.

"Don't worry about it, buddy," said Dad. "You'll have plenty of other games. This is just one." Dad reached over and handed Evan a mint. Dad always kept a tin of Altoids in his pocket. "The peppermint will help settle your stomach."

After a few more incidents—none with throwing up, at least—Evan figured out what was happening. He was sensing the disconnect, the mismatch between what someone was saying and what they were really feeling. He got better at managing it, so now the sensations became more like a warning.

What he could never figure out, though, was why he never noticed that his dad had been lying to them the whole time.

CHAPTER TWO

MARTHA HOOVER

Martha Hoover, the number-one real estate agent of Haddington, Virginia, wished that the new family would do something, well, *interesting*. To be honest, the Pao family, currently ensconced in her car, was going to be the most exciting addition to Haddington in quite some time.

Their name, Pao, for starters. When Martha first received the text message from Elaine Pao, the mother, she had tried to figure out how to pronounce P-A-O and landed unsteadily on *pay-oh*. That was wrong, and thank goodness she never said it out loud, in front of the family. She didn't want them to think she was some kind of uncultured fool. It was pronounced *pow*, like the sound effect in a *Batman* comic.

Celeste, the older child, was starting high school and, like every other teenager Martha knew, was firmly attached to her phone. Since she was dressed completely in black, Celeste seemed to have dissolved into a blob in the back seat. Martha had heard that Chinese parents were stricter than most, but Celeste seemed to have free rein to answer in grunts and not make eye contact from the back seat. *That's a lesson, Martha*, she told herself. *Don't make assumptions about people.*

Evan was in sixth grade. Ms. Pao said he was twelve, and Martha judged that he was just starting a growth spurt, being thin and gangly. What Martha really liked were his eyes, bright and curious. He seemed like a boy who paid attention. He had a phone, but did not seem surgically attached to it. When she offered him a granola bar and a bottle of water, he accepted both and said thank you. He also took the granola bar his sister had refused and put it in his pocket for later. She noticed that he did not get crumbs in her freshly vacuumed back seat, which earned him many points in Martha's book.

It would be *so interesting* if one of the Paos would do something different, like speak to one another in Chinese or take off their shoes when they got in the car. It'd just be something to bring up at dinner or at church, a way of casually establishing that she'd met the new Chinese family early on. *Not to make fun of them*, Martha admonished the imaginary listeners in her head. She'd heard plenty of that "Chinese flu" and "kung flu" business, and while she had not spoken up about it, she silently judged the people who said it as childish and coarse.

Since the Paos remained so stubbornly normal, Martha focused on highlighting the best parts of Haddington. This was part of her work—not just showing houses but showing the town to the rare out-of-town visitor. The "good" grocery store, the swinging bridge, the bakery that had been featured on television for their buttermilk pie. She showed them the statue in the town square, but she did not mention that the figure was supposed to be a Confederate soldier. They might not like that. She wanted the Paos to like Haddington, to make it their home for good. Towns thrived with new people.

Celeste cackled at something on her phone, and then showed it to Evan, who smiled politely.

"What's so funny?" asked Martha, trying again to engage the teenager.

"Nothing." As quickly as she had opened up, Celeste closed up into her black cloud. Ms. Pao shared a look with Martha, half apologizing, half sympathizing. Martha imagined that many of their conversations at home were like this.

"Do you like baseball, Evan? My sons played here." A dusty baseball field passed by the window, with sponsor signs along the outfield and a green wooden scoreboard with the words HADDINGTON LITTLE LEAGUE, EST. 1957 written across the top in white paint. Martha hoped they noticed that she had a sponsor sign in the outfield.

"You didn't ask me if I played," said Celeste, emphasizing the *I*. Martha knew that the girl was jabbing at her, indirectly implying she was a sexist for not asking both of them. It wasn't that, for heaven's sake. She just didn't seem like a team sports kind of person.

"Well, do you?" Martha asked.

"No," said Celeste.

"Celeste is a musician," said Ms. Pao. "She plays the cello."

"Played," Celeste corrected. She enunciated the *d* so it became its own syllable. Play-duh. "Played the cello."

"I played," said Evan. "Baseball, that is."

"He played baseball. He was the pitcher," said Ms. Pao. Martha could not quite bring herself to refer to her by her first name, Elaine. It seemed too personal, too intimate.

"Oh!" Martha grabbed on to this idea like a lifeline. "The teams have already been picked since it's so late in the spring, but I'm sure someone would take you on. A team always needs a good pitcher. I bet we could find you a spot."

"He said he *played*." There it was again. Play-duh. "He didn't say he liked it," said Celeste. "He threw up."

"Celeste," said Ms. Pao, her voice stern.

Martha decided to change the subject, and nodded at a tree covered in pink flowers. "That's the dogwood. That's the official tree *and* flower of Virginia."

"I know what the official motto of Virginia is," said Celeste. "It's *sic semper tyrannis*. It means, 'thus always to tyrants.'" She held her phone out to Evan. "It's on their flag."

"The flag has a *dead person* on it?" said Evan.

"Huh," said Martha. She had never thought of it in those terms, but the Virginia flag had one person standing with his (or her?) foot on the body of a dead or at least very ill man. She thought quickly. "Other states have flags with people who are deceased on them. I believe the Washington state flag has George Washington on it."

"Not at the moment of his death," said Evan, distressed. "Not in the middle of a murder."

"It's symbolic," said Ms. Pao. "The man represents tyranny or a tyrant. He's been defeated." She cleared her throat.

13

"Do dogs like dogwood? Is that where its name came from?" Martha silently thanked her for changing the subject away from the subject of dead people on flags.

"I don't think dogs like it any more than any other tree. My own dog, a yorkiepoo, has been trying to climb the beech tree in my backyard to catch squirrels and birds for ages."

At the mention of a dog, Evan sat up. "You have a dog? What's your dog's name?"

They were at a stoplight, so Martha brought out her phone and pulled up a picture of Moxie. "Seven pounds of pure energy," she said.

"She's cute," said Evan. He handed the phone back as the light turned green. "I wish I had a dog."

"Under the terms of the lease, you can have . . ." started Martha. Ms. Pao caught her eye and shook her head. Martha let her sentence fade away. No dogs, got it.

"Daggers," said Celeste suddenly. Martha had to catch herself from swerving the car at this sudden announcement of a weapon from the frowny teenager.

"Pardon?"

"Dogwood is hard and good for making daggers. Skewers. Arrows. *Dag* eventually became *dog*."

"Cel is really good at finding information on the Internet," said Evan.

Ah, well one had to seize opportunity where one found it. "You're going to fit in so well here!" chirped Martha. "Are you interested in other weapons? We could go take a closer look at the cannons in the town square if you want."

"No!" That was the boy, emitting a yelp. He tried to recover. "I mean, we should save that trip for later."

"The house," said Ms. Pao. "Thank you for showing us around town, but I think we're ready to see the house."

The house. Well, yes. There was that. Martha could tell that the Paos had money, or had once had money. They had driven a Mercedes-Benz to the office, for goodness' sake, and not an old one, either. Evan was wearing those socks that her son had wanted, but she had said no after seeing how much they had cost. Twenty dollars—for a single pair of socks!

But when Martha had asked for their budget for renting a home, she had tried not to look surprised. Even for Haddington, it was a very low amount, and as of right now, there was only one house that fit the budget and was convenient to the schools. The Shumley house.

From the outside, it wasn't so bad. A yellow house perched

on a corner lot, with a slanted roof, a large front window. It was when you looked more closely that the house started to lose its appeal. The concrete stairs leading up to the front door, chipped from years of wear and tear, for instance. They looked like broken teeth. The roof really should be replaced, too.

"Oh!" said Ms. Pao. "It's, it's so . . . cozy!" The Paos had driven separately, after going back to the office to retrieve their car. They were approaching the house cautiously.

"That's the nice word for tiny," said Celeste. Martha wanted to strangle her.

"It's not large," said Martha. "But that also means small heating and air-conditioning bills."

Ms. Pao looked at the house, folded her arms, and sighed. "May I have a moment with you?" she asked. Martha nodded and the two women moved a few steps into the yard.

"Are you sure there aren't any other homes within the budget I gave you?" asked Ms. Pao.

Martha shook her head. "I'd need a little more flexibility on the rent," she said.

Ms. Pao held up a finger and then walked back to the children and had a private conversation behind the car. Martha wasn't sure what they'd be talking about. Were they going to decide not to move to Haddington after all? Were the children going to help with rent? After a moment, though, Ms. Pao poked her head over the roof of the car. "This is the best house," she said cheerfully. "Let's go see the new house, kids!"

Martha opened the front door, hoping that the lemon-scented air fresheners she had put in the day before had worked. The house now smelled like someone had been smoking lemon-scented cigarettes. She tried to discreetly fan the air and focused on the positives.

"Look at that window!" she said, pointing to the large living-room window. At least she had that to feature. Light flooded into the room, almost making the floating dust motes look pretty.

It didn't take long to show the rest of the house. On the opposite side of the living room from the big window, toward the back of the house, hung a pair of swinging doors that led to the kitchen. A hallway on the far side of the living room led to the three bedrooms.

Evan opened the door to the first bedroom on the right. "This room has two doors."

"The other one leads to the kitchen. A direct line to a midnight snack," said Martha.

Evan nodded. "Sold."

"It means your room is essentially a hallway," said Celeste.

"Maybe it will be your room," said Ms. Pao to Celeste. Martha cheered on the inside.

"I might like it, anyway," said Evan. "Beeline to the kitchen and room to escape."

They returned to the living room to sign paperwork. Lacking any furniture, the children spread out on the carpet while they waited as Ms. Pao signed the lease. Evan pulled out the second granola bar and offered half to his sister.

A low, menacing growl filled the air, a vibration like being near a beehive. Celeste and Evan popped up from the carpet and ran to the window, just in time to see a low black car with flames painted on the sides roar down the street and up the hill.

"Who is that?" asked Evan.

Martha closed her eyes. It was Charlie Griggs. She supposed that every town had a family like the Griggses, a family that had lived in the town as long as anyone could remember, always brushing right up against the law. The car, which also had a skull and crossed knives painted on the doors and the words NO MERCY spelled out underneath, was the latest test of traffic laws. The town had no law on overly loud cars, but at the last town council meeting, people had begun to talk of one. No one mentioned the Griggs car, specifically, but it was the only one Martha could think of.

The car stopped suddenly at a two-story house with blue shutters. Charlie jumped out of the car, and slammed the door. The sound cracked like a gunshot.

"Is that our neighbor?" asked Ms. Pao. She had just signed the last paper.

Mrs. Hoover flushed and looked through her purse. "Some people, they really do up their cars," she said. "Though honestly, I don't know how he affords it. Charlie Griggs has a hard time staying employed." Perhaps it was something indiscreet to say, but she wanted to say something, to make it clear she was on their side. Evan turned and stared at her for a moment. When Martha looked back at him, he nodded solemnly, as if she had passed a test.

Martha prided herself on being a people person, and looking at their faces, she could definitely sense that the car had changed the mood in the room. Were they afraid? The boy, especially, had seemed intimidated by the car. "He's harmless, though," she assured them. "More of an occasional annoyance."

CHAPTER THREE

EVAN

After Mrs. Hoover left—and it seemed as though she would never leave—Celeste pressed her body against the front door and locked it twice, once with the button in the doorknob and then with the chain. Celeste was thin, which you could tell even when she wore bulky layers of black clothes, so she gave the impression of a slender black line pressed against the door.

"What are you doing?" asked Evan. They still had boxes and bags to bring in from the car.

"She knows, doesn't she? That comment, 'I don't know how he affords it.'" Celeste covered her face. "It's starting again."

"She didn't know how to say our name," said Mom hesitantly. "If she'd heard about Michael Pao in the news, she would have known how to say our name." Mom began walking in a tight circle. "She doesn't know, does she, Evan?"

Mom had promised to only ask Evan about what he was feeling when the issue was *really important*. The problem was right now, everything seemed really important. When the real estate agent had said this house was the only one within their budget, Mom had asked Evan if this was really the only house Mrs. Hoover could show them. Maybe she was trying to squeeze more money out of them. Mrs. Hoover, Evan told his mom by the side of the car, really was doing her best for them.

"She doesn't know," Evan agreed. He gestured toward the house with the NO MERCY car. "She was just talking about that guy. NO MERCY—what's that about?"

"It's how the world treats everyone," Celeste muttered. "That's why we're here."

"The real estate lady was nice," said Evan. "She really did want to show us another house, if we had more money."

"Which we don't."

"It wasn't about Dad. It was just a thing she said." His stomach rumbled. "You don't suppose any food got left behind, do you?"

"How can you think about food at a time like this?" said Celeste.

"We have to eat," said Evan. He opened the fridge and some of the cabinets. He found a can of green beans, two years past its due date. He wasn't that hungry.

"I just don't want to have moved all this way, just to have ... *issues* ... start over again," said Mom. "This was supposed to be our fresh start."

A fresh start. Evan liked the sound of that, like a freshly made bed, clean smelling sheets. No hostility. No sideways looks. He could just be Evan, again.

Uncle Joe was the reason they had come to Haddington, Virginia, out of all the places they could have gone to. He had lived in Haddington for eight years. He had come through when a hurricane knocked out all the power, while he was working for the electric company, and then, according to Uncle Joe, he forgot to leave. Uncle Joe liked to fix things. He had a toolbelt that jangled with tools, but if you got down to it, he said, he really needed only three things.

"A screwdriver, duct tape, and pliers will get eighty, ninety percent of your jobs done," he said. "Maybe you need a hammer or a drill sometimes." Uncle Joe was tall; he didn't even need a chair to get to the ceiling fixtures. He wore his hair in a long, graying ponytail. Mom said he was a Chinese hippie. Evan had never met anyone like him. Uncle Joe went through the house, calling out solutions to problems. Replace the washer on the leaky faucet. Throw some baking soda on the carpets to freshen them up. Get some drywall to fix a hole in the wall. Uncle Joe seemed to be enjoying himself.

Mom asked him to check on the car after what the man at the garage had said. Uncle Joe took the car out, came back, and shrugged. "Car seems fine," he said. "Plenty of tread on Lincoln's head." He became mildly horrified that Evan didn't know what he was talking about. "You use an upside-down penny to check on how much the tires are worn down. If you see all of Lincoln's head, it's time to get them changed."

"I don't drive," said Evan. "Even Celeste doesn't drive yet."

"No one should drive before they know basic auto maintenance! The boy needs to learn about home repair, and cars," he said to Mom. "What have you all been doing out in California?!"

"Not home repair," Mom said gently. "He can learn now." Evan decided this was not a good time to mention that Mom had only recently started letting him use a paring knife to cut up apples.

"He needs to know how to do these things," Uncle Joe said to Mom. "How to fix things. You can't keep him a little boy who can't do things for himself." Evan supposed he should feel insulted. Uncle Joe was saying he was soft. That's what one of the other parents on the baseball team had said, after the incident on the mound. Evan needed to toughen up. "The world is a hard place," said one of the dads. "Get used to it."

For Evan, though, someone like Uncle Joe, who said exactly what he thought, was the easiest kind of person to be around. His insides and outsides always matched. Evan liked that. Also, he had brought over a barbecue dinner with a whole set of sides—baked beans, macaroni and cheese, cornbread. He'd even brought an apple pie. Evan had two slices and then Mom said he should stop. If he was still hungry, he could have a carrot. Who could eat a carrot after apple pie?

Uncle Joe noticed another problem. The door from Evan's bedroom to the kitchen kept swinging shut, like a ghost had decided that the door should stay closed.

"We'll take out the hinge pin and bang on it," said Uncle

Joe. Evan tried to pretend that he knew what a hinge pin was, but he didn't fool Uncle Joe. Uncle Joe sighed and told Evan to watch. He took out a hammer and small thin piece of metal, and then tapped on the piece that held the door to the frame until a pin, which held the hinge together, came up and out.

They took the pin outside, and then Uncle Joe handed Evan the hammer and told him to put a dent in the pin, about one-third down from the top.

"You want me to put a dent in a perfectly straight pin?" said Evan. He wanted to show Uncle Joe that he was thinking, not just blindly following orders, even if he didn't know what was going on.

Uncle Joe sighed. "Yeah, that's what I said. Now, do you know which end of a hammer to use or do I need to show you how to do that, too?" He didn't say it in a mean way. Evan laughed and picked up the hammer and hit the pin. He was about to hit it again when Uncle Joe stopped him. "No need to go overboard. Now we're going to put it back in where it came from, but with the bend in." They went back inside and Uncle Joe let Evan put the pin back in the hinge. The door stayed open.

"Ha!" Evan was amazed. Who knew that you needed something to be crooked to work properly? Uncle Joe explained that the friction from the bend in the pin kept the door where it was put.

"Stick with me," said Uncle Joe. "I'll teach you everything you've been missing. You guys weren't going to learn anything, living the way you did."

"We could have learned without . . . everything else," said Celeste.

"Well, there's nothing we can do about that. This is a nice town," said Uncle Joe. "You'll be okay here."

"Can you take a look at the back door before you leave tonight?" Mom asked Uncle Joe. "The lock has a problem." The back door was old; instead of a regular window, it had a screen covered by a ladder of glass pieces that could be cranked open or closed.

"Does it lock?" asked Uncle Joe.

"The button doesn't stay in," said Mom. "So I put a chair under the knob." Evan nodded in agreement. He'd nearly tripped over the chair coming from his room to the kitchen. "I can put the chain on, but a door lock is better," said Mom.

"It's a peaceful neighborhood," protested Uncle Joe. "I don't

26

even lock my door, to be honest. It's just because you're new here. Once you settle in, you won't lock your door, either. It's practically an insult in this town."

"But why take a chance?" asked Mom. "It can be a peaceful town and I can have a locked door."

"So peaceful that the school is named *Battlefield*," Celeste said. That had been a surprise. They had gone for a walk after they had unpacked the car and found the school Evan would attend. Battlefield Elementary was all one story, made of pale, red brick. The school sign in the front said, LEARNING WINS AT BATTLEFIELD.

"What's wrong with calling a school 'Battlefield'?" asked Uncle Joe.

"It sounds like they're preparing you for war. You wouldn't name a school, I don't know, Gladiator Stadium," said Celeste. "Combat Zone Middle School."

Uncle Joe threw his head back and laughed. A gold tooth glinted in the back of his mouth. "You're something," he said. "Taking everything so literally. No one's sending you guys to war."

"It's worse," Evan said. "In battle, at least there are people on your side. I'm being sent into school, alone."

27

"I'll come with you," Mom said quickly. "I'll go with both of you, meet your teachers."

"Don't you have to go to work, too?" asked Celeste. Evan silently thanked Celeste for thinking of a reason why Mom could not come to school for more than a minute. Evan couldn't think of anything he wanted less than Mom coming with him to class. Uncle Joe had arranged for Mom to start working as an office manager in a dentist's office.

"True," said Mom, disappointed. "They do start rather early there."

"Let 'em be, Elaine," said Uncle Joe. "They'll make friends. People here are nice. Everybody gets along."

"Ha," said Celeste. "Ha-ha. Have you been to a high school in the last twenty years?"

"I'm serious!" said Uncle Joe. "I've never had a problem here. Go along to get along. You'll be fine."

"What does that mean, go along to get along?" asked Evan. The guy with the car, thought Evan. NO MERCY. He didn't seem like he wanted to get along with anybody.

Uncle Joe scratched his head. "I guess it means, make a point of being agreeable. Maybe you don't always get your way, but it's important to get along."

28

"Mom says, 'put your head down and don't cause trouble,'" said Evan.

Uncle Joe nodded. "Same thing. Except mine is better." Mom laughed and poked Uncle Joe, like they were still kids, fighting. It was nice to hear Mom laugh with someone other than Evan and Celeste. They had been their own little circle for so long now, clinging to each other for safety, for comfort. Now they were letting Uncle Joe in.

After Uncle Joe had left for the night, Celeste offered her own advice as they brushed their teeth in their new-to-them bathroom, checkered in mint green and eraser pink tile.

"You need to go in like a boss," said Celeste. "Whatever you're actually feeling, don't show it, unless your feelings are, *I am a boss.*" Celeste spit in the sink. "Look at Uncle Joe. He thought you should know how to use tools, which means the boys here probably do. They probably go hunting, too. Back home, everyone was okay with you being Mr. Sensitive, but it's probably not going to fly here."

"Mom said you shouldn't call me that," Evan reminded her. "Mr. Sensitive." That was the nickname Celeste had landed on after the cause of Evan's headaches and nausea had been discovered.

Celeste stepped to one side so Evan could get to the sink. "I'm telling you for your own good. I don't want you to get pushed around. Again." She rinsed out her toothbrush. "Speaking of which, we need a strategy about Dad."

"What about Dad?"

"What are you going to tell people if they ask you about Dad?"

"Maybe no one will ask."

"Not right off the bat, but it's going to come up. And you and I have to say the same thing."

"We could say Mom and Dad are divorced. That's true. Almost." Mom had filed the papers.

Celeste narrowed her eyes. "Maybe we should say that Dad is dead."

"What? No! Why would you say that?" Even more shocking than the idea was the casual way Celeste said it. She could have been saying anything, like what flavor of ice cream to choose at the store.

"He's not coming back, Evan! He left us, he's a jerk, end of story. What's wrong with you?"

Evan dipped his chin down. "Saying that someone is dead when they're not is bad luck." No one had actually ever told

30

him this, but how could it not be true? It was like wishing someone was actually dead.

"Yeah, well we certainly don't have any bad luck now," said Celeste, her voice laden with sarcasm. "Moving to this nowhere town in this stinky little house." She put her hands on her hips. "How come your little ol' feelings-o-meter never went off for Dad?"

Evan had wondered the exact same thing, many times. What had he missed? Why hadn't he sensed anything about Dad? Maybe if he had, he could have stopped Dad before things got worse.

"I don't know," said Evan. He lowered his voice, murmuring the one idea he had been nursing. "Maybe it's all a big misunderstanding."

"Oh right," said Celeste. "Maybe all of our neighbors just *happened* to lose the money they gave to Dad to invest, and then he *happened* to disappear around the time the police showed up."

Dad had worked for a venture capital firm, helping to identify the next big idea. It meant long hours and working dinners. Dad said it was like going on first dates all the time, meeting people and getting to know them quickly, which he loved to do. One day, Dad came home with an idea that was too "small potatoes" for the firm, but he was excited about it. "Socks that change color when you move!" said Dad, laughing. "Another way to encourage activity in kids! It's genius. I'm going to make our own little investment group, with the neighbors."

Mom frowned. "What if this loses money? That would make things awkward."

"It's not going to lose money! The neighbors are going to be thanking me, and the ones who don't go in are going to be furious!" Dad always had that enthusiasm, that way of talking that made you believe in him, in yourself.

For weeks, maybe months, it was all the neighborhood could talk about. Michael Pao was so generous, so amazing, to bring this opportunity to them. When Dad brought home prototypes for Evan and his friends to try, Evan became the most popular kid at school.

But then one day Dad didn't come home at all. They checked the hospitals, called the highway patrols for reports of an accident involving Dad's car. Nothing. Evan called Dad's phone over and over, hoping he would pick up. Then Mom realized Dad's passport was missing. When the FBI showed up, Mom went from worried to angry. Dad had betrayed them all,

Mom told Evan and Celeste. He'd taken the money and left them all high and dry. Evan hadn't heard that term before, *high and dry*, but he quickly figured it out. It meant broke.

Sometimes Evan replayed the last memory he had of his dad, searching for clues. Dad had come home from work as Evan was getting ready for bed. That wasn't unusual. Dad looked a little tired and rumpled, but that wasn't unusual, either.

"How's it going, Evan? Homework done?"

"On time, on point, and on to the next thing," said Evan. That was their routine. They high-fived and then Dad grabbed him and hugged him.

Sometimes Evan wondered if he was getting too old for hugs, but that night felt okay. "I love you, you know that, right?" said Dad. Dad said embarrassing mushy stuff like that; he said his dad never said those things, so he was making up for it. Evan said he did, and then went to bed. That was the last time he saw his dad. It was the last time the neighbors saw their money.

What had he missed?

Evan recapped his toothpaste. "Maybe. Maybe Dad..." That was as far as Celeste would let him go.

"Evan," said Celeste. "Don't."

"Don't what?" asked Evan.

"Don't hope," said Celeste. "Not when it comes to Dad. He doesn't deserve your hope."

Evan hoped he'd feel a twinge when Celeste said that—something to show she didn't mean it. But nothing. Her insides matched her outsides.

CHAPTER FOUR

MAX

Mr. Hawthorn, the principal, brought the new boy in right after Mrs. Norwood's lesson on improper fractions. An improper fraction was a fraction where the number on top was bigger than the number on the bottom. Max was just amused by the term *improper*. It seemed like an etiquette word, not a math word.

When the new boy walked in, though, Max let go of all math-related thoughts. They did not get new students that often, and as far as Max could remember, they had never had an Asian student.

Max had never been the new kid. He'd lived in Haddington his whole life, and so had his dad, and his dad before him, and so on. Everything was familiar to him—the people, the

35

streets, the buildings. He knew where the honeysuckle smelled sweetest in the spring, and where the roads flooded when a hard rain came. He couldn't decide whether it was comforting or boring to know a place so well, down to the cracks in the sidewalks.

Max tried to imagine being the boy and seeing what he saw, twenty-two unfamiliar faces looking back at him. What did he notice about the classroom first? The board on Thomas Jefferson and James Madison? The light over Mrs. Norwood's desk that flickered constantly? The windows that overlooked the fields behind the school?

"Class," said Mrs. Norwood. "Please welcome Evan Pao." Mrs. Norwood had been a teacher for so long that she had taught Max's dad back before she was married, when she was Miss Hayes. Now she was going to retire after this year. Mom liked to say that Mrs. Norwood was old school, meaning that she had very specific ideas on the right way to do things. "He is from California. Welcome to the class, Evan."

California. Max had been to Disney World, the Outer Banks, and Washington, DC, but not California. That was a whole other world. He inched forward, trying to see how California might make Evan different.

"Thank you," said Evan. He waved shyly to the class. Then he straightened up and lowered his voice. "I mean, hello."

"We are reading *Rascal*," said Mrs. Norwood. "Do you know it?"

Evan shook his head. "Would anyone like to tell Evan about the book?"

Julia raised her hand. "It's about a guy who gets a raccoon as a pet." Julia was the girl who always raised her hand because she always knew the answers. She wore her straight brown hair in a braid, and looked at you with serious gray eyes.

"Sterling North," Mrs. Norwood corrected. "The author, Sterling North, is recounting a year from his childhood when he had a pet raccoon."

"Do you have a pet?" Julia asked Evan.

Evan shook his head. "I wish I did. I want a dog." Max nodded. He had a dog, Chessie. His family had always had dogs, but Chessie seemed to belong to him.

"Do you have the China virus?" Max watched Evan as he took in a breath and stepped back, away from the class. Max did not have to look to know who had spoken. Brady Griggs. The class groaned.

"Seriously?" asked Casey.

"Brady," Mrs. Norwood said. "That's a terrible question. Of course Evan doesn't have it."

"I mean, I wouldn't come to school if I had a virus," said Evan, reasonably. "Of any kind."

Max and Brady had once been friends, close friends even. Once, when Max got to bring one friend up to DC for a Nationals game, he'd chosen Brady. But they'd been growing apart lately, partly because Brady made comments like that. Brady had gotten an early growth spurt, and was already close to the size of Mr. Welsh, the gym teacher. It seemed like the whole thing had made him angry. Pimples had erupted across his face, and his clothes constantly strained against him, too small and tight. They weren't enemies. Max just kept a careful distance.

"It's called COVID-19, not China virus, you dummy," said Taylor. Taylor and Julia were best friends, an opposites-attract situation. While Julia was quiet, Taylor was outspoken and opinionated, as wild as her tangly red hair.

"It came from China, didn't it?" demanded Brady. Max and Brady had had this same argument about this when the pandemic started. Max hadn't known what to say, exactly, except

38

it seemed mean to say China virus. Taylor, however, did know what to say.

"Diseases come from all over the place," said Taylor. "And you're just using that name to be a jerk. People have *died* because of comments like that." She looked to Mrs. Norwood for confirmation. Mrs. Norwood nodded, slightly. Max had remembered his dad talking about attacks against Asians in the news, but it seemed more abstract then. Now Evan was here.

"Class," said Mrs. Norwood. She clapped her hands in a pattern—1! 2! 1-2-3!—and the class responded in kind, as they had been taught. "Settle down. Let's not give Evan such a terrible first impression of the class. We don't shout at each other or call each other names." Max looked at the clock. They had fifteen minutes until lunch.

"Who would like to be Evan's partner and show him around?" Mrs. Norwood asked.

Max raised his hand, along with just about everyone else in the class. Everyone except Brady. *Pick me*, Max silently begged. *Pick me.* What would it be like, Max wondered, to be a stranger, to have things unknown and to be unknown? He might never know what that was like, but maybe Evan could tell him.

Mrs. Norwood scanned the room. Max knew she wouldn't pick a girl; Mrs. Norwood would think that was improper. Max wiggled his hand in the air and smiled, the one that teachers found hard to resist. He knew he was one of Mrs. Norwood's favorites. He didn't try to be, he just was. Part of it was his family—his dad was the police chief and his brother Clark had been student body president the year he was in sixth grade. His mom was PTA president one year. That year, she was at the school as much as the teachers, it seemed.

Mrs. Norwood caught Max's eye and he knew a split second before she said it. "Max Baldwin," she said. "You'll do a good job, won't you?"

"Yes, ma'am," said Max. He was already scooting his desk over, making room for Evan. "Absolutely."

In the course of a twenty-eight-minute lunch, Max took it upon himself to fill Evan with as much on Mrs. Norwood and Battlefield as he could. Of course he had a lot of questions for Evan, but it only seemed fair to give him the lay of the land first. That included the long list of Mrs. Norwood's likes and dislikes ("Just tell her you want to go to the University of Virginia—she loves that place"), what to avoid in the cafeteria ("Do not, under any circumstances, buy the fish they serve on the third Wednesday of the month"), and Battlefield Day.

"What," said Evan, "is Battlefield Day?"

The lunch table was full today. The students had their choice of seating among three tables, but everyone wanted to sit near Evan. "Nobody give it away," Max warned them. "I want to see what he thinks." He faced Evan and said, "What do you think we do on Battlefield Day?" Evan turned his face up toward the ceiling, thinking.

"Is it like an outdoors day, where you go outside and have activities?" asked Evan. "They called it field day at my old school. We had races and the school rented a bounce house, stuff like that."

"That's a good guess," said Max. "We do go outside. But it's not to do regular stuff."

"Think about the *battle* in *battlefield*," said Casey, trying to help. Casey was one of Max's best friends. Max elbowed him.

"Oh, so you guys do something about wars?" said Evan. "Battles and wars?"

"Yeah," allowed Max. "So which war do you think we study?"

"Um . . . World War II?" Evan guessed. Max shook his head. "World War I?"

"Older," hinted Max. "In the 1800s."

"The Civil War?" Evan got it. Max nodded approvingly. "That's the one when Lincoln was president, right?" asked Evan.

Some of the kids politely stifled giggles. Asking if Lincoln was president during the Civil War was like asking if kickball was the game that involved kicking and balls. Didn't everyone know that? Max tried to help him out.

"Mrs. Norwood is a huge Civil War buff. On Battlefield Day, we all get to dress up like it's the Civil War and live like the people did then." Max paused and tried to gauge Evan's reaction.

"Mrs. Norwood has volunteers who set up stations on secret codes and medicine and all sorts of stuff," said Taylor. "We get to spend the whole day outside and see what it was like back then."

"We eat stuff from the Civil War, too," said Daniel. Daniel was the kid who could draw anything. Max wondered if Evan had noticed the dragon Daniel had drawn on his notebook.

Evan raised his eyebrows. "Food *from* the Civil War?" he asked.

"I mean, not directly from the Civil War, but food like what they had during the Civil War," Daniel clarified.

Max studied Evan's face as each person contributed a detail. He hoped that Evan was excited. He tried to imagine what it would be like for someone who had not grown up in Haddington, or even in Virginia, to learn about Battlefield Day for the first time. Evan barely knew about the Civil War. Was it weird? Max had lived here his whole life; he couldn't tell.

"Ohhhh," said Evan. "Well, that sounds like fun. I mean, anything that gets us outside, right?" The people at the table murmured approvingly. Max relaxed.

"It's more fun for the boys than the girls," complained Taylor. "The girls have to wear these hot dresses that go all the way to the ground." She and Julia had parked themselves at the edge of the table.

"Mrs. Norwood says we can dress like soldiers, but she doesn't really like it," said Julia. "The girls only get to pick from the leftovers when the boys are done."

"Mrs. Norwood has a huge trunk of costumes for Battlefield Day," explained Max. "You can have anything you want, as long as it's gray."

"You *can* be a Yankee," said Daniel. "But Mrs. Norwood isn't going to help you."

"So . . . you don't actually act out a battle?" asked Evan, taking a bite of sandwich. "Too bad. That would be cool."

Here was the thing about being the new person. Max had never questioned what they did on Battlefield Day. It was just what they did—the cooking, the costumes. But then here came Evan, and right away, he saw things differently. Why didn't they reenact a battle for Battlefield Day?

"Yeah," Max agreed. "It would be."

Max saved one surprise for Evan at the end of the day. When they walked out of school, Mom and Chessie were waiting for him.

"Come here, girl!" called Max. Mom let go of Chessie's leash, and she sprinted across the blacktop and leapt into his arms. This was the game they played every day. She tilted her head up and licked Max's chin. Max waved to his mom and kept walking. Mom would walk home with Jacob, his little brother.

"Your mom just let go of the leash like that?" asked Evan. He seemed more astonished about this than Battlefield Day. "What about kids with allergies? Or don't you worry that she'll run off?"

"It's a tradition," said Max. It had never occurred to him

that Chessie would do something other than what she was supposed to do. "She's very well behaved."

"I can see that," said Evan. He shook his head. "It's just one more way things are different here." He pulled out a package of Skittles from his pocket and offered Max some. Max took three.

"Like Battlefield Day?" asked Max.

"Among other things," said Evan. He seemed to have something to say, then stopped. Instead, he picked out two purple Skittles and popped them in his mouth.

"You can ask me anything," said Max. "Really."

"I feel kind of dumb," said Evan. "Like I was supposed to know this, right? War. The Civil War."

"Naw," said Max. "Go on, shoot."

"I know that the Civil War was the war between the states, the North versus the South," said Evan.

"That's right," said Max. "From 1861 to 1865." He gestured around them. "Lots of fighting, right around here."

"They fought over slavery," said Evan.

"Some people will try to tell you that it wasn't, but it was," said Max. "My daddy showed me the declarations the Southern states made when they seceded from the United States. They all talked about slavery and the right to own people as slaves."

45

"*Secede*," said Evan. "That's a word you don't hear every day."

"It's like *recede*, like the tide. So, when the Southern states seceded, they formed the Confederate States of America. Anything with that word, *confederate*, has to do with the South. The boys in gray. The Northern states, led by Lincoln, were called the Union, and their soldiers were called Yankees. Their stuff tends to be dark blue." Max tried to remember how he came to know this, but he couldn't. He just did.

"It's funny that Yankees became a Northern versus Southern thing. Everyone was a Yankee when we were fighting the British during the Revolutionary War," said Evan.

Max stopped walking, which meant Chessie stopped walking. "You know, I'd never thought of that. We were all Yankees, huh?"

"Don't think too hard. You might hurt yourself." Brady ran up and pretended to karate chop Max. "Hi-yaaaa!"

Max hoped that Evan hadn't seen the karate chop. "Hiya, Brady," he said, trying to pretend that Brady had said hi the same way. He took a deep breath. "We were just talking about Battlefield Day and all that. That's a big deal in your family." Max wondered what Evan had thought of Brady's comment

46

earlier in the day. Maybe just giving Brady a chance to brag would put things to right.

"'Course it is," said Brady. "Jubal Griggs was known for being a crack shot and a soldier's soldier." Max noticed that Brady was only looking at him, as if Evan did not even exist. But Evan did not seem to notice.

"Oh, so what side was he on?" asked Evan. "The Union or the Confederacy?"

Max cringed. Evan was just trying to show that he was getting the terms straight, but his comment infuriated Brady.

"What side? What side?" Brady roared. "Do you know where you are, boy? The Confederacy, of course! The capital of the Confederacy was in Virginia! Do you even know American history?"

"I'm just, I'm still figuring things out," said Evan. He stuck his hand out. "No hard feelings, okay? I just thought that if you were that proud, he might be on the Union side because they're the ones who won the war." He laughed a little. "I mean, I have a lot to learn, but I know that much."

Max resisted the urge to cover his face with his hand. This was not going well.

Brady stared at Evan's extended hand. "Huh." He didn't shake. Max wanted to shake *him*, but then Brady started rubbing Chessie behind the ears, which was her favorite spot. "Who's a good girl," crooned Brady. "Chessie's a good girl. Chessie probably knows more about the Civil War than Evan." Chessie wagged her tail.

"Hey," said Brady to Max. "Have you decided who you're going to be for Battlefield Day?"

"Not yet," said Max, keeping his words short.

"You have a Confederate general in your family! That'd be an easy decision for me." Brady gave Evan a sideways glance. "Not sure who you're going to be." Brady gave Chessie a last scritch behind the ear and walked away.

"Sorry," said Max, after Brady disappeared from view.

"*You* didn't do anything," said Evan.

"Still," said Max. "I feel kind of responsible for him. He's being kind of a jerk."

"You guys talk about the North and the South, the Confederacy and the Union, like it was all just a few years ago. It's not the same for me. I keep having to check that I'm not mixing things up." Evan leaned down and scratched Chessie behind the ears, the way Brady had done it. She leaned up against his shins. Chessie liked Evan, Max could tell.

"I'm sure he'll get over it in a bit," said Max. "He just gets a little hot sometimes."

"I'm not trying to make him mad." Evan seemed slightly exasperated. "I just got here. I'm trying to get along with everyone."

"Brady can be nice," said Max. "When I was seven, I got my tonsils out. Brady got worried, so after bedtime, he climbed out his bedroom window, shimmied down a tree, and came to my house to check on me." Max smiled at the memory, seven-year-old Brady's face popping up in his window.

Evan did not laugh. He closed his eyes and pinched the bridge of his nose with his fingers.

"Are you okay?" asked Max. Evan looked like he was going to be sick.

Evan spoke while keeping his eyes closed. "I'm okay."

"Do you need to sit down? Put your head between your knees?" That was Max's mom's solution when someone wasn't feeling well.

"Just tell me the truth," said Evan. He opened his eyes.

"Why are you telling me this about Brady? Do you think he's nice now?"

Max hesitated. "Now? No. Not exactly."

"Okay then," said Evan. Suddenly, he was back to normal, walking, talking, and not acting like he'd just been hit by a baseball bat.

"Brady is not an easy person to get along with," said Max. "I'm not saying you have to be best friends, just that it'd be good if you could find a way to get along. He actually lives pretty close to you. If you're on the corner, in the Shumley place, then Brady is just up the hill and across the street, kind of catty-corner from you."

Evan opened his eyes. "*Catty-corner.* You mean *diagonal?*"

"Sure," said Max. "Though *catty-corner* rolls off the tongue a whole lot easier. *Diagonal* sounds so, you know, mathematical."

"Brady's family, they have a car right? One with a skull painted on it, really noisy engine?" Max's heart sank. Charlie's car was not going to help Evan think any better of Brady.

"It's hard to miss, isn't it?" said Max.

"Yeah, then I know which house," said Evan in a matter-of-fact tone. "We saw the car the day we moved in." Of course the car had not helped make Brady seem more appealing. How could it? It was not a welcoming first impression.

Max remembered one time Charlie had played hide-and-seek all afternoon with Brady and Max when they were little. Charlie had seemed so fun, so kind that day. But now Max had to wonder, was the day memorable because it was rare?

CHAPTER FIVE

EVAN

"Do you want to come to my house and help me fix a toaster?"

This was how Evan knew that he and Max were becoming friends. It wasn't just the invitation, which Evan accepted immediately. It was that fixing a toaster sounded like a totally excellent, if strange, idea.

Max's house was closer to the school, an old-fashioned two-story house with a porch in the front. Max showed Evan around the house. The word that came to mind for Evan was *full*. Paintings and photographs covered the walls. The furniture was dark and heavily carved. Every flat surface seemed to have a book or a small sculpture or another photograph.

"How long has your family lived here?" asked Evan, thinking that it took a long time for a house to become so full. His own house had just gotten up to the bare minimum. Sofa, kitchen table and chairs, beds. One piece of art hanging on the wall.

"More like, has my family ever *not* lived here," said Max. "This house belonged to my dad's parents, and his parents before him, and so on." He pointed to a gray-and-white photograph, faded with age, of a young man and woman. "That's my great-great-great-great-great-grandparents." He pointed to another photograph of a man with a beard in a military uniform. "That's Davenport Baldwin. He was a general on the Confederate side."

"A general," said Evan, impressed.

"Yeah, yeah," said Max, waving his hand. "A general that no one has ever heard of. Let's get a snack." Chessie followed them into the kitchen.

Max's mom was in the kitchen, looking at an iPad. "Hey, boys!" she said cheerfully. "You must be Evan. You here for a snack?" Max's mom had blue eyes and a wide smile, just like Max.

"Do we still have the snickerdoodles?" asked Max.

"With your brothers? No." She smiled apologetically at Evan. "It's like the *Hunger Games* around here with three boys. How about an apple and some cheese sticks?"

53

Max took two apples out of a bowl, and then grabbed some cheese sticks from the fridge. "Do we get something if we fix the toaster?" he asked.

"You get toast," said Max's mom. Evan laughed. He could see where Max's good nature came from.

The two boys sat on the floor of the porch and examined the toaster. "The toaster won't stay down," explained Max. "It heats if you hold it in place, but who wants to do that?" He picked up a screwdriver to open the toaster when Evan stopped him.

"Have you tried just shaking out the crumbs first?" he asked. "It gets pretty messy inside." Evan knew this from first-hand experience. When they were moving, he'd picked up the toaster and accidentally tipped it over. A shocking amount of dried crumbs had spilled out.

"Good point," said Max. He turned the toaster upside down and shook it gently. Brown crumbs spilled out on the floor. The more Max shook it, the more crumbs spilled out. Max tested it again. Now the handle stayed down.

"That was easy," remarked Evan. "A crumb must have gotten in the way or something." He felt slightly disappointed that his idea had worked.

Max grinned and waved a screwdriver in the air. "Want to take it apart, anyway?"

"Will your mom be mad?"

"Nah, not as long as we don't make a mess," said Max. He brushed the crumbs into the cracks between the floorboards. "And my dad will be glad that we're not playing video games."

When Max said *dad*, Evan felt a pang. Dad had had similar feelings about video games. *No one's going to change the world playing games.* Evan pushed the memory down and forced himself to smile.

They took the toaster apart and admired the mechanics inside—the springs and the baskets that held the bread. Evan pressed the lever down and they watched it catch. Max got a canister of compressed air and blew out even more crumbs.

"There's probably bread crumbs from the last century in there," said Evan.

"No doubt," said Max. "I think this belonged to my grandma." He jumped up. "You play ball? I heard you play. Pitcher, right?" Max laughed at Evan's look of surprise. "You're in a small town, now. I know all your secrets. Mrs. Hoover goes to our church."

"Oh boy," said Evan, trying to pass off Max's comment as a

joke. He tried to think quickly. "So you know that I'm actually an international spy."

"Yes, Haddington is the perfect place for you to blend in. Not," said Max. "I can't think of a worse place, actually." He opened a wooden box on the porch and pulled out two baseball gloves and a ball. Max handed Evan a glove and threw him the ball.

Evan smiled faintly. The first day he had gone to school, it had taken him a minute to figure out what seemed different. At his old school, the students had been a mix of white, Black, Asian, Latino, and Middle Eastern. In this class, he was the only student who wasn't white. There were a few Black students in the school, but none were in his grade, and as far as he could tell, no other Asian students were in the whole school. When he thought of it, it made him feel weirdly aware of his skin, as if it were a shell separate from his own being.

Evan tried to keep the conversation light. "That's the genius part," explained Evan. "No one expects the kid who sticks out." He tossed the ball back and shook his arm out, trying to warm it up gently.

"Hiding in plain sight! I love it," said Max. He aimed the

ball high into the air. A fly ball. Evan started to put his glove up to catch it, the proper form, and then switched to a basket catch. Smooth.

Max whistled. "You're good. You fixin' to play ball? I bet I could get you on my team."

Fixin'. They had just fixed the toaster, but that's not what Max was talking about. *Fixin'* meant planning, Evan decided. Evan shook his head. "I just play for fun." He threw the ball back. "Adults kind of ruin things."

"Well, that's true, at least sometimes," said Max. "My dad coached when I was little, but then he got promoted to chief and now he's too busy."

There it was again. Dad. Evan wondered if it was weird that he wasn't saying anything about his own father. He didn't think Max was prying. He wasn't saying these things to get Evan to say something. Max was just talking about his dad.

But secrets. A small town knew all your secrets.

Maybe it was best to try to head things off. "My dad's not around," said Evan. He threw the ball back.

Max nodded sympathetically. "It happens. That's nothing unusual around here."

But does anyone have a parent who disappeared? wondered Evan. Max threw the ball back, harder this time, and Evan caught it with a satisfying *thwack* in the pocket of the glove.

"So, I got to ask, what do you think of this?" Max held out his arms, gesturing widely.

"Think of . . . your front yard?" asked Evan.

"No! This town! This place. You ever live somewhere that had a Battlefield Day?" Max's eyes were wide, curious. "You didn't have anything like this in California, right?"

"Not specifically," admitted Evan. Whenever they had talked about American history in school, it had seemed kind of remote because it had happened across the country. Now it was practically on top of him. "But it's interesting. I mean, you said there are costumes and we get to be outside. And we get to eat."

"I wouldn't get your hopes too high on that point," said Max. "It's food during a war."

"There's no situation that can't be improved with food," said Evan. "That's my experience."

"We have good food here," said Max. "If people in the South know how to do one thing, it's how to cook and eat."

"You can't beat the Chinese," said Evan. "There are eight

major types of Chinese food. We literally ask *have you eaten* as a greeting."

Max laughed. "I didn't know that."

"Really? Based on *allll* the Chinese people who live here, I'm surprised," said Evan, joking.

Max tossed himself the ball. "But do you like it here? What do you think?"

Evan didn't answer right away. He didn't want to be rude, but he wanted to be truthful. "I haven't been here long enough to decide," said Evan. He was thinking about Brady. But Brady wasn't the whole town. There was still Max and the other kids in school. Being close to Uncle Joe. People here waved to each other when a car drove by. He liked that. "But I'm *fixin'* to like it," he said, repeating Max's word.

"Now you sound like one of us," said Max.

Evan may have started to sound like the people in Haddington, but that didn't mean he could understand the people in Haddington all the time. Mrs. Norwood kept talking about something called *air looms.*

"It's only for people who have 'em to share. Don't worry about it. No one's expecting you to have one," said Max.

"An air loom."

"That's right."

"You've got one?"

"You've seen my house, right?" said Max.

Evan had searched back through his memory, trying to picture a loom in Max's house. He couldn't remember seeing one, but to be fair, he couldn't rule out the possibility, either. Max's house had a lot of stuff. Maybe Mrs. Norwood was into really authentic Civil War clothes.

She was also, apparently, into scribes.

"Evan, I've been thinking that you should get a special role for Battlefield Day. What would you think of being a scribe?" she asked Evan one day when he had gone up to the desk to ask about a writing assignment. She folded her hands and looked at him intently. She drew out the last word. *Scriiibe.*

"A scribe?" Evan could feel a wave coming on, a mismatch. Mrs. Norwood was acting all enthusiastic, but she seemed to have something underneath. But maybe he just didn't understand the word *scribe.*

Mrs. Norwood turned red. "It's just that, Battlefield Day has a certain look, and I thought, um, that it might be more comfortable for you to have a, um, behind-the-scenes role." Her voice strained to a whisper, which of course, made the class look up and stare at them.

Evan felt the room start to turn funny. Mrs. Norwood was telling a lie, but maybe not a serious one. "What would a scribe do?" asked Evan.

"A scribe would, um, describe what is happening. Like a historian. You write down what happens that day so we have a record. You can interview people and write down what you see. And you can make a report to the class!"

That definitely did not seem as good as being a soldier. "I think I'll just stick to being a soldier," Evan told her politely. "That seems like the best."

She didn't seem to hear him. Mrs. Norwood wrote the word SCRIBE on an index card, folded it in half, and put it inside his hand. "You think about it," she said. "Don't decide right away, but I think you'll see it makes sense."

Evan walked back to his desk. Max handed him a bag of cereal. They were testing for iron in the cereal, using magnets to draw out tiny bits of iron.

"What was that all about," whispered Max.

"I'm still not sure," Evan whispered back. "Mrs. Norwood said I should think about being a scribe for Battlefield Day."

"A scribe?" said Max. He wrinkled his nose. "That sounds boring. Why would you be a scribe when you could be a soldier and do stuff?"

"Beats me," said Evan. "I'm going to say no, but first I have to pretend to think about it."

"Maybe she likes the way you write," said Max. "Maybe she thinks you'd make a good report."

Evan rubbed the bridge of his nose. A scribe was not part of the action. A scribe described the action. Mrs. Norwood had been acting like she was doing him a favor, but something did not match up. *Did that mean*, Evan wondered, *that he was doing her one?*

At the end of the day, Mrs. Norwood announced that it was time to share the air looms.

Max showed him what he brought. He reached into his backpack and pulled out something wrapped in a T-shirt. He peeled back the layers and produced a round metal object, about the size of a small dinner plate. "It's my great-great-great-great-great . . ." He stopped and did some mental counting. He nodded, satisfied he'd gotten it right. "Grandfather's canteen."

"That's a canteen," said Evan.

"Yes, it is," said Max. He slowed down his words.

"A canteen is not used to make cloth," Evan said, making his words as slow as Max's. "Not a loom."

Max looked away and covered his mouth for a moment. When he turned back to face Evan, his face was perfectly serious. "Evan," he said. "Are you under the impression that everyone is bringing in looms to make cloth today?"

Evan was starting to get the feeling that he should be grateful—very grateful, in fact—that Max wasn't outright laughing at him. "Kind of?"

"Oh boy," said Max. He took a deep breath and looked away. "How do I explain this?"

Max managed to explain without making Evan feel too much like a fool. H-E-I-R-L-O-O-M. Heirloom, not *air loom*. Mrs. Norwood explained it this way when she called the class to order. "Today we begin our preparations for Battlefield Day," she said. "By bringing in items from home connected to the Civil War that have been passed down in our families."

"I won't go first," said Brady. He had a larger box, which

he picked up and rattled. "Just because it will make all of your things look so minor in comparison."

"That's very gracious of you, Brady," said Mrs. Norwood dryly. "You might have to wait a bit for your turn." Evan glanced around the classroom and realized how many class-mates had brought in boxes or shopping bags or thick brown paper envelopes. It felt like every hand around him went up in the air, begging to be called on.

Evan folded his hands and looked down at his desk. Even if he had understood the assignment, he would not have had anything to bring in.

Sophia went first. She had a black-and-white picture of a man in uniform, holding a sword. The picture was on a flat piece of metal. My great-great-great-great-great something or other, James Woodall," she said.

"Do you know what battles he was in?" asked Mrs. Norwood.

"Maybe . . . Gettysburg?" she said.

"Don't guess. Do you know what side of your family he's from?" asked Mrs. Norwood. Sophia shook her head. Mrs. Norwood sighed. "It's not enough just to bring in something. You should know the story, your connection to the object. The Civil War was the first war to be photographed a lot, the

64

battles and the soldiers. It's not like today, with digital cameras. Photographers had to bring all of their equipment, heavy, heavy equipment, in wagons." She held up the photo. "This is called a tintype. It's on metal, see? And the image is still sharp."

Max leaned over to Evan and whispered, "I told you she's really into this. She knows more about these heirlooms than the people who bring them in. She can tell you their stories."

He was not going to get a story, Evan realized. He felt embarrassed by his deficiency. Even though Mrs. Norwood and Max had said it was okay not to have anything, it did not feel good to be the only one without something to share.

Mrs. Norwood laughed at a letter that Daniel brought in, from his great-great-great-great-great-grandmother telling her husband that she was "as fat as a pig," Mrs. Norwood pointed out that she probably didn't want her husband to worry that she was going hungry while he was away since food supplies sometimes ran low in Virginia. Even Max's plain old canteen had a story.

"These bullseye canteens were for the Union soldiers," she told him. "Your great-great-great-great-great-granddaddy probably took it off a dead Union soldier." Some of the class cheered, as though the war was still happening. Weren't they all supposed to be on the same side now, reunited as one country? Wasn't this all in the past?

Then Evan got it. This was why Mrs. Norwood had asked him if he wanted to be the scribe. This was why Max told him not to worry about the heirloom. This is what Brady meant when he said *I don't know who you're going to be.* His classmates had real connections to the Civil War. They were touching the things their ancestors had touched, knowing the stories their families had known. He was watching the action, but not part of it. It was Mrs. Norwood's way of telling Evan, maybe in the kindest way she could, that he did not belong.

He lifted his head and by sheer accident, caught Brady's eye. Brady smiled harshly and then shook his head, slowly and deliberately. He wiggled his box deliberately. That, more than anything, made Evan feel worse than anything.

He'd just have to try harder, thought Evan. Try harder to belong.

CHAPTER SIX

CELESTE

"You fixin' to eat that?" Evan asked Celeste. They were both standing in front of the fridge and he was practically breathing down her neck. Evan was a maniac around food.

Celeste shook her head and turned to face Evan, still blocking his access to the fridge. "Evan, why are you talking like that?" Normally, she might have let the whole thing pass by, but her nerves were already on edge.

"Like what?"

"Like what? Like you're some deep-fried cornpone dude from around here. We don't say *fixin'* and if we were to say fix-*ing*"—Celeste made sure to go hard on the second syllable—"we would mean that we are in the middle of repairing some*thing*."

"Geez, who died and appointed you the head of proper pro-nunciation? I'll say what I want," declared Evan. "Uncle Joe said to go along to get along. There's nothing wrong with talk-ing like the other folks."

"Folks?" Celeste nearly fell over. "The only time you should say *folk* is when the word *music* comes right after, and you've got an acoustic guitar in one hand." She shook her head. "We're not from here."

"I know that," said Evan. "I just like the way it sounds."

"You're not fooling anyone," said Celeste.

She had not meant for her words to cut so hard, but they did. Evan seemed to deflate. "Tell me about it," he said. Celeste felt guilty for a second, but then again, Evan already had a new best friend. What did he have to complain about?

"Tell *me* about it," said Celeste. "This boy at school? He *thinks* he likes me. Ugh. His name is Luke. He follows me around, telling me how pretty I am and how he likes my long black hair and how I must be so smart and I'm not like the other girls, blah blah blah."

"Gee, an admirer. Poor you," said Evan.

"Except he doesn't know anything about me! I'm just an idea to him. A thing. He doesn't know what I like, or what I believe in. I'm just some weird idea of being cool and exotic to him. We've never even really had a conversation."

"At least he's not asking if you have the China virus," said Evan sulkily.

Celeste put her hands on her hips. It was one thing for her to give Evan a hard time, but an entirely different issue if someone else did it. "Someone actually said that? You should tell the teacher."

Evan hesitated. "She was right there, and she told him not to say that. But he still hasn't actually been going out of his way to be nice. Not like you and that boy."

"It's the same thing, Evan. A person who hates you without knowing you is the same as a person who likes you without knowing you."

"One situation seems slightly more pleasant than the other," Evan pointed out. "I would accept being superficially liked. Why don't you make some real friends if that's your problem?"

"I'm not getting attached to anyone here. I mean, what's the point if I'm just going to leave after graduation?"

"In a couple years," Evan pointed out. "That's a long time. You're going to be lonely a long time if you don't try."

"I'm looking into graduating early," said Celeste. That was a slight exaggeration. Her counselor had mentioned that she might be able to get accepted early to a college if she did well on the SAT.

"If you say you're fixin' to graduate early, people will know what you mean," said Evan stubbornly. He reached around Celeste, grabbed a bowl of spaghetti out of the fridge, and took it with him to his bedroom. He didn't even stop to heat it up.

Uncle Joe came over for dinner, but the air between Evan and Celeste was still tense. Evan sat at the dinner table and scowled at the dishes Mom had put out. Celeste decided that she would try to put on a good face, just to be different from Evan.

"I just got my first biology test back," announced Celeste as she helped herself to some rice. "Highest grade in the class. My plan for world domination has begun."

"Good job," said Mom. "Evan did well on his test, too. In math." Evan looked surprised.

"The test I had this morning?" he said. "I haven't even gotten the test back." Mom put a big scoop of rice in her mouth

70

and then shook her head, indicating that she couldn't talk with her mouth full. Celeste smelled a rat.

"Did you talk to Evan's teacher today?" Celeste asked.

Mom took her time chewing and swallowing. "I've been checking in with her by email." She didn't look at either one of them directly. "She says you are a good student, in case you are wondering," she said to Evan.

"When's the last time you talked to her?" Celeste asked. "Or emailed her?"

"Mmmm . . . this afternoon?" Mom dabbed her lips with her napkin.

"And the time before that?"

"This morning?" She made it sound like a question, like she wasn't sure, but Mom knew, Celeste was certain of that.

"Mom, have you been emailing Evan's teacher twice a day?" Celeste set her fork down. A horrible idea occurred to her. "Have you been doing that to my teachers, too?"

"No!" Mom was indignant. "I've only been writing to them once a day. Not all of them write back, I must say. Very disappointing."

Celeste and Evan exchanged looks. "Mom, you shouldn't be writing to the teachers without telling us," said Celeste. "We

71

don't want to be *those kids*. The ones whose parents are a big pain. If we need your help, we'll ask." Uncle Joe grabbed a napkin and covered a smile.

"I just want you guys to get off on the right foot here. There's been a lot to get used to." Mom looked like she might start crying. Celeste felt guilty, but only guilty enough to stop being mad on the outside. She was still steaming on the inside.

"They're going to be okay," said Uncle Joe. "They're good kids. Don't be one of those drone parents."

"The term is *helicopter parent*," said Celeste. Uncle Joe laughed.

Mom took a deep breath. "I was planning on cutting back, anyway."

"Well, you need to just stop. No wonder my English teacher keeps asking me if I'm okay." Celeste leaned back in her chair and shook her head.

Evan had been quiet this whole time. He was, apparently, getting madder.

"When you were emailing Mrs. Norwood, did she tell you that tomorrow is the last day to share heirlooms?" asked Evan. "Did she tell you that everyone had something to bring in about the Civil War except me and that she wants me to be a scribe?" His voice rose with each word until he was yelling.

"Jeez, Evan, calm down," said Celeste. "It's not a big deal. Mom said she would stop."

"Yes, it is!" said Evan. "At least I'm trying!"

"That sounds like an awful assignment," said Celeste. "What if you had a classmate who was Black? What would they bring in?"

"I don't know," said Evan miserably. *What was worse, to have nothing, or to have the evidence of an awful past?* Celeste wondered. Her thoughts were interrupted by her uncle thumping the table.

"But you had relatives who fought in the civil war!" thundered Uncle Joe. "Both of my grandfathers, your great-grandfathers, fought for the Nationalists." Uncle Joe shook his head in disgust. "No relatives in the civil war!" he repeated. Evan was too shocked to respond, which Celeste approved of. At least Uncle Joe had shaken him up a bit, gotten him out of his pout.

Celeste tried to clarify. "He means the American Civil War, Uncle Joe. Not the Chinese Civil War." Uncle Joe did not seem to hear her.

Uncle Joe waved a spoon around for dramatic effect. "A civil war is a civil war. Neighbor fighting neighbor. Brother against brother. If your teacher didn't specify American Civil War, you should talk about the Chinese Civil War. It will be good for class discussion. Isn't that what they do these days? Compare and contrast?" Uncle Joe cricked his neck. "More people should know about Chinese history, anyway."

"You don't know Mrs. Norwood," said Evan. "This is, like, her life. She only cares about the American Civil War."

"I'll let you bring in one of my grandfather's grenades," said Uncle Joe. "Your great-grandfather. It was called a potato masher grenade. There was this handle so you could throw it . . ."

"We cannot, can NOT, bring in weapons," Celeste interrupted. "You can get expelled for that." Did they allow weapons in school when Mom and Uncle Joe were young? Maybe Battlefield Elementary was more descriptive than she thought.

"I don't want to bring in a weapon from the Chinese Civil War," said Evan. "I'll just look stupid." Uncle Joe looked disappointed. Now it was Celeste's turn to feel irritated. Uncle Joe was only trying to help.

Celeste blew her hair out of her face, pushing out her lower lip and aiming a huge puff of air toward her forehead. "It's stupid; this whole thing is stupid. If I were you, I'd strut in there and say, yeah, I don't have anything and I don't care. We have our own history. Thousands of years of history."

"Stop giving your brother a hard time," said Mom. Evan had stopped eating and bowed his head. Ugh, Mr. Sensitive got away with everything.

"You're so dumb! You know there aren't Chinese people in the Civil War! Why do you want something you can't have?" Now Celeste was shouting, too. There were so many things they wanted that they couldn't have. Their old house, their old friends, their old way of life. Why add one more thing?

Evan poked his chin up. "You don't know that! You can't prove a negative," Evan said, his voice matching hers. Uncle Joe slid slightly back away from the table and mouthed *wow*. "Boy, this sounds like some of the fights we used to have," Uncle Joe said to Mom. "Remember the time you threw a *mántou* at me?"

"Celeste, you need to be the better person here. Stop giving your little brother a hard time," said Mom in a singsong voice. Even in the moment that Mom was defending Evan, Celeste had to snicker. The one thing Mom definitely did not say was that Evan's wish wasn't stupid.

"I'm going to google 'Chinese' and 'U.S. Civil War' and get zero results," Celeste said, pulling her phone out of her pocket. They were not allowed to have phones at the table, but it was time to finish off this pointless discussion. "Have you ever heard of a googlenope? That's when a search is so dumb"— she made sure to pause on this word—"that you get zero results."

Celeste was fully confident in her ability to search for any idea, any fact. She started typing on her phone, windmilling her arm in a totally unnecessary gesture to press ENTER. She held the phone toward Evan before the search completed, just to make a point.

Evan did not look defeated, though. He stared at the phone, his eyes growing wider. Celeste turned the screen back to see what he was looking at.

"Whoa," said Evan. "Whoaaaaaaa."

A black-and-white photo. A man in a slouch uniform, decorated with big buttons and a wide belt. It was like so many pictures Celeste had seen in history books at school, with one major difference.

"That's an Asian soldier," said Evan, taking the phone from Celeste. He zoomed in on the bottom. "His name was Joseph

Pierce. He fought for the Union. He was in the infantry, whatever that is. He was born in China."

Uncle Joe crowded in to take a look. "*Infantry* means the foot soldiers," he said. "The hard-core part of the military." He took the phone from Evan and stared at the screen with one eyebrow raised, skeptical. "That's not a Chinese name, though."

Evan took the phone back and scrolled down some more. "He was brought to the U.S. from China by a Connecticut ship captain. He adopted him. That's why his name doesn't sound Chinese."

"Can I have my phone back, please?" Celeste enlarged the photo to get a better look at his face. He had a determined, impatient stare, as if he needed to be somewhere else. "You guys can look this up on your own phones." She looked back at the search results. "There's more than just Joseph Pierce," she announced.

Under normal circumstances, Evan would have been a pain about Celeste being wrong. It would have been a whole thing. But now he was staring at his own phone. "I can't believe it," said Evan. "We fought in the Civil War." He touched the screen.

"I don't think we're related to any of these soldiers," said Mom. "We would have heard, right? My grandparents came over in the 1960s." She didn't say anything about Dad, but Celeste knew. Her dad had come to the U.S. as a little boy in the 1980s.

"It doesn't matter," said Evan. He was practically giddy. "We were here. We were here. I get a story."

CHAPTER SEVEN

MAX

Casey Plummer was one of Max's best friends, mostly because they were the two most athletic boys in the class and kept up a friendly rivalry between them. In the past, Max was usually the faster one, while Casey excelled in events involving grip strength and hand-eye coordination. Casey had recently undergone a growth spurt, much to Max's dismay, giving Casey another advantage in their post-lunch recess games of three-on-three basketball and flag football. Max made a habit of measuring himself every Sunday morning, to see if he might have a growth spurt starting, but so far, no luck.

Casey was the best quarterback for flag football, a game they normally played on Thursdays after lunch. Max suggested that Evan could be the other quarterback, which everyone agreed to. "We could use another quarterback," said Casey. "Makes the teams more even." Casey's comment didn't surprise Max. Casey liked a good competition. What did surprise him, though, was that Casey made Brady his first choice. Brady was not a first-round pick for these games—he was kind of slow and yelled at other people.

"I'll take care of it for you," Brady said to Casey after they were done picking teams. Max's ears pricked up. What was Brady talking about?

"What's going on?" Max asked Casey. Casey shrugged. "He really wanted me to pick him for my team," said Casey. Max was Evan's first pick, along with Taylor, Julia, and Jack.

Taylor counted off seven seconds for Casey. After an incomplete pass, Casey managed to move the ball downfield on two short passes connecting to Daniel, who added some yardage on foot before getting his flags ripped off, first by Max and then by Julia. On the fourth down, Casey lofted the ball into the end zone to Brady, but the ball sailed through his hands. Max still couldn't tell what Brady's deal was. Brady didn't even seem that upset that he couldn't catch the ball, which was unlike him.

Now it was Evan's team's turn to have the ball. Brady lined up in the center, across from Max who was hiking the ball to Evan. The plan was for Max to run a buttonhook pattern for Evan to throw to. If that didn't work, Evan's second option was Jack, but Jack would have to get past Casey, which was tricky.

"One . . . twothreefivesixseven," shouted Brady.

As soon as the second syllable of seven, *ven*, came out of his mouth, Max hiked the ball and took off. He thought Brady might make a move for him, but Brady charged across the line of scrimmage, straight for Evan instead. Max looked over his shoulder. Evan backed up a few steps, launched the ball downfield. Brady still came charging at him.

Max stopped running and turned to watch. *Brady's going to tackle Evan*, was Max's first thought. *Brady is going to crush Evan* was his second. Brady was about six inches and twenty to thirty pounds bigger than Evan. The whole purpose of flag football was to eliminate tackling, and that's exactly what Brady was about to do.

"Evan! Look out!" shouted Max.

Evan looked as surprised as Max felt. Brady opened his arms wide, lowered his body, and lunged straight at Evan's knees.

Evan seemed to levitate almost straight into the air. Of course, that was impossible. People can't levitate. *Or can they?* Evan jumped, tucking his knees in, leaving plenty of space underneath him. Brady went crashing face-first into the dirt while Evan landed to the side unharmed. The ball thudded in the dirt.

Almost immediately, a crowd formed. Taylor turned away, said something to Julia, and they both burst into giggles. Something about Brady, Max guessed.

Brady rolled over in the dirt. A brown smudge started on his chin, and then continued down his shirt and pants. Alex offered him a hand up. Brady batted it away.

"Flag on the play, repeat first down," announced Max, jogging up with the ball under his right arm. "You okay, Ev?" Evan nodded.

"What's the call?" asked Jack.

"Tackling," said Max. He didn't name names, but he didn't need to.

"It wasn't a successful tackle," ventured Alex.

"Only because Evan outsmarted Brady," said Taylor, pretending to jump in the air. Julia and Taylor started laughing again.

"It wasn't on purpose," said Evan. "It just seemed like the best way to get out of the way." Evan sounded defensive, as if he was the one who had done something wrong.

"Attempting to tackle counts," said Max. "Y'all saw it, right? We have to call it." He said the words without looking directly at Brady. A few heads nodded in agreement. Brady folded his arms.

"He cheated," Brady declared. "Pretty sure that was an illegal move."

"You're the one who made an illegal move," said Taylor. She said the exact words Max was going to say. "As in tackling? During flag football?"

"Shut up, Taylor," said Brady. "You don't know what you're talking about."

Mrs. Norwood's whistle interrupted them, signaling the end of recess. Normally, there were sighs of disappointment when the whistle sounded, especially on a pretty spring day like this one. This time, though, no one complained or tried to sneak in one more play. No one wanted to deal with Brady when he was mad.

Max thought Evan might have been shaken up after the game, but he seemed fine. Happy, even. When Mrs. Norwood asked for the last volunteers for heirlooms, Evan raised his hand.

Evan? Maybe he had been hit. In the head. Mrs. Norwood raised her eyebrows, and called on him.

"It's not an heirloom, exactly," Evan said shyly. "But it's really cool." He pulled out a single sheet of paper and held it up. It was a picture of a soldier in a Civil War uniform, but the soldier was Asian. "I found out last night there were Chinese soldiers during the Civil War. The American Civil War. This soldier's name was Joseph Pierce."

Every single person in the class was paying attention. Hands started to go up in the air. Mrs. Norwood, knower of all things related to the Civil War, seemed stunned.

"Did he speak English?" asked Sophia.

"That's not a Chinese name, though, right?" said Jack.

"Is he related to you?" asked Alex.

Evan shook his head. "I wish, but my mom is pretty sure we're not related to any Civil War soldiers because of when we came to this country."

"He looks like you," said Daniel.

"How did he end up in the United States?" asked Julia.

"He was adopted," said Evan. "A ship captain brought him to the U.S. from China when he was little, probably because there was a famine in China. At least that's what my uncle thinks."

"*Famine* means an extreme shortage of food," said Mrs. Norwood. "The Irish potato famine is a famous example. Lots of people from Ireland came to the U.S. in the years before the Civil War because of the famine."

"So he probably spoke English," said Julia. "Did he survive the war?"

"I don't know," said Evan.

"You expect us to believe this?" That question was from Brady. "You gotta be making this up." It was the same tone Brady had used when he accused Evan of cheating in flag football.

"I'm . . . I'm not," Evan stammered. But the class quieted down, contemplating Brady's point. Anything was possible with some photo editing, thought Max. And why hadn't Evan brought this in sooner? Then Max felt embarrassed by his thoughts. Evan was his friend.

"You've never heard of this, right?" Brady pressed Mrs. Norwood. "You've been studying the Civil War for years and years, longer than the war itself. He's making this up 'cause he wants something to share."

"I know a lot," said Mrs. Norwood. "But I'm not too proud to say that there are things I don't know. I know there were

Black soldiers in the Civil War. The United States Colored Troops made up one-tenth of the Union Army, but I don't know anything about Chinese soldiers." When Mrs. Norwood said "Colored Troops," Evan felt a start. Would Chinese soldiers have been in those troops?

"What about the Confederate Army?" asked Casey. "Did the Confederate Army also have Black soldiers?"

"My understanding is that the Confederacy allowed the enlistment of Black soldiers in the last month of the war," said Mrs. Norwood.

Taylor made a noise. "So, when they made Black people soldiers, they basically admitted that they needed Black people to win the war they were fighting to keep Black people enslaved. So much irony."

Mrs. Norwood didn't respond. She reached for the photo, and then withdrew her hand. "Evan, maybe you could go to the library and find out more. Just to be a little more certain." She cleared her throat. "Any other questions before we move on? Evan is going to get back to us. Really extraordinary information," she said, half to the class, half to herself.

"But that means I don't have to be a scribe," said Evan. "I can be a soldier, right?"

86

"I never said you had to be the scribe, but yes, I can see why now, the role of soldier would seem especially appealing." Mrs. Norwood looked over at the clock. "Well, that took longer than I had planned, but it's worth it. Let's work on vocabulary before it's time for . . ."

"Wait," said Brady. He held up his box. "I haven't gone yet. You can't just stop after Evan."

"Oh yes, right. My apologies. Does anyone else have something to share?" asked Mrs. Norwood. No one else raised their hand.

"Very well," said Mrs. Norwood. She leaned against her desk and rubbed her eye. "You may share, Brady."

Brady rubbed his hands together. "You guys won't believe what I have," he said, lifting up the flaps of the box. "It was worn by my great-great-great-great-great-grandfather on my father's side." He reached both hands into the box and pulled out something heavy and wooden. "Jubal Griggs. You can look him up. It's the leg they made for him after his leg got blown off at Chancellorsville. His left leg." He stood the leg up on the desk, and the class could see the shape of a foot, calf, and knee, with long flat metal pieces holding them together. At the top was a cuff with laces to attach the leg to the person.

"My dad said that his grandmother said he could do chores as well as anybody," said Brady.

Mrs. Norwood said that an artificial body part was called a prosthetic. "At a time when men were defined by their ability to do physical labor, instead of working at a computer," she said. "Prosthetics were very important to help soldiers feel whole. And amputations were very common during the war."

Daniel raised his hand. "My uncle has prosthetic legs because he lost them in Afghanistan. Sometimes they give him rashes, but he says they're okay. He used to get phantom pain, too."

"What's phantom pain?" asked Taylor.

"It's pain from a body part that isn't there anymore," said Daniel. "It's like your brain's wiring gets tricked."

Mrs. Norwood nodded. "Does anyone else have a question or comment for Brady?"

Brady made the leg take a few thumping steps across his desk. The class watched the foot roll along the top, the hinges squeaking slightly. *Ka-chunk, ka-chunk, ka-chunk.* But no one had any more questions.

"I liked Evan's thing the best," said Julia quietly, as if trying to explain their silence. "It's something different than the same old stories."

"If it's true," said Brady.

"It is true," said Evan.

"We can have old stories and new," said Mrs. Norwood. "There's room for both."

But did the old stories stifle the new ones? Max wondered.

CHAPTER EIGHT

EVAN

Normally, the house was empty when Evan got home from school. Today, though, Uncle Joe was there, working on the back door. Uncle Joe waved, holding a screwdriver in his hand.

"Job finished up early for once," said Uncle Joe. "Thought I'd take care of this door before your mom worries any more about it. Trying not to have to rehang it, though. That'd be a pain."

Doors were hung? This was news to Evan, but he wasn't going to share that with Uncle Joe. "I helped my friend Max fix a toaster the other day," Evan told him.

"That's the stuff," said Uncle Joe. "Right there. That's how I got my start. Fixed an oscillating fan when I was about your age. People are too willing to throw things away these days."

"When you were my age, like, when you could bring a grenade to school?" teased Evan. This was the closest he'd ever felt to Uncle Joe, thinking that Uncle Joe had been his age once.

"How'd that go, anyway? Did the kids like the photo? Pretty great find." Uncle Joe kept working as he talked. He pressed the button on the lock, but the door still opened. "I think I'm going to replace the doorknob and the keeper."

"Some of the kids thought the photo was a fake," said Evan.

"No!" said Uncle Joe stoutly. "It's not."

"How do you know?" asked Evan. Maybe Uncle Joe wanted that piece of history as much as Evan did. "Why didn't we know about Joseph Pierce if he's real?"

"C'mon," said Uncle Joe. "There's lots of things I don't know. Doesn't mean they're not real." He began packing up his tools. "But we're going to settle this right now." He stuck the chair back under the door. "You're in luck. This is one of the days the library is open and I have a friend who can help us."

"The library? You have a friend at the library?" Evan followed Uncle Joe out to his truck. Libraries, in Evan's mind, were for adults who wore sweater vests and flat brown shoes.

Uncle Joe, with his long gray hair and deep pockets of duct tape and screws, didn't quite fit this idea.

"Of course!" Uncle Joe seemed slightly insulted by the question. "I use the library and I get to know the people who work there. You think I'm some sort of ignoramus?"

"No, not at all," said Evan hastily. "I guess it's a side of you that I didn't know about."

"'I am large, I contain multitudes,'" said Uncle Joe, starting up the truck. "You know Walt Whitman?"

"Is that your friend's name?" asked Evan.

Uncle Joe laughed. "Walt Whitman was a famous poet. But since his words bring me comfort, sure, let's go with that. He's a friend, too."

Uncle Joe parked the truck on the town square and they walked over to a low brick building. The library was spare, with a black-and-white linoleum floor and off-white walls. A few ceiling fans twirled from the ceiling. Uncle Joe waved to a man sitting behind a tall wooden desk. He had a name tag—G. Lavers. Mr. Lavers reminded Evan of a sparrow, with bright brown eyes and quick movements.

"Those books you wanted are coming back next week," he told Uncle Joe. "I'll call you when they're ready for you. And did you want to renew those books you've had out? They're almost due."

"That's great," said Uncle Joe. "But we're here for something else today." He gave Evan a small push forward. "This is my nephew, Evan, and he's on a research mission. Evan, this is my friend, George Lavers."

"Call me George," said the librarian, shaking Evan's hand. George's mouth fell open as Evan explained what he was looking for.

"That's amazing!" he said. "I can definitely help you. The Civil War is always a subject of interest around here." He pointed out back toward the square. "You know, we have a public hearing going on in one of the meeting rooms right now about the statue of the Confederate soldier in the town square. There's talk of taking it down."

"C'mon. It's history," said Uncle Joe.

George snorted, nicely. "If only. Except, what do you know, about two dozen towns in Virginia all got the idea to put up Confederate statues around the same time, in the early 1900s, including Haddington. All at the courthouses. Pretty amazing coincidence, huh?"

"I don't get it," said Evan. "Isn't it a coincidence, I mean?" Uncle Joe looked equally confused.

"Civil rights protests were happening around that time," said George. "Protesting things like the segregation of street-cars. The NAACP was founded. The statues were put up to intimidate. To show what, or who, was valued, and who was not."

"Maybe." Uncle Joe didn't look convinced. Evan nodded slightly. It seemed possible. He'd seen clips of what happened during the civil rights protests of the 1960s—attack dogs and fire hoses used against protestors. A statue could be another way of saying no, of denying people rights.

George shook his head. "It was no accident, those statues going up when they did. It takes a lot of effort to pay for and plan a statue, especially on a courthouse lawn, the place where many people seek justice." George emphasized the last word. "But enough of me on my soapbox. Sorry, I get carried away sometimes when people say that statues are history. It is, just not the history they're thinking about." He turned to his computer and began tapping. "So, we need to figure out if Joseph Pierce is the real deal?"

Evan nodded, though he was imagining what it would be like to see the statue and feel unwanted or unable to get a fair shake. What if he came to school one day, and there was a big statue of Brady Griggs in the front? It wouldn't make him feel welcome. Uncle Joe leaned forward on the counter so he could see the screen as George typed. Evan rose up on his toes to get a look, too.

"Well!" George said. "A quick Google search shows that he's mentioned on multiple websites, including some pretty reputable ones, like this one from the National Park Service. But, I personally like to see some primary sources to be one hundred percent sure." George stopped typing and stared at the screen.

"Me too," said Evan, though he was racking his brain to remember what that meant. Primary sources were things like newspapers and firsthand accounts. So wasn't a photo a primary source? His head was spinning.

"Mmmm. I have an idea. The library has a subscription to a genealogy database." After a few more moments, he turned the screen and showed Evan what looked like a really messy chart. He tapped the monitor. "Look here. This is the census from 1880. It shows that a Joseph Pierce lived in Meriden, Connecticut, with his wife and daughter, and that he was born in China, and his parents were born in China."

Evan ran his finger along the screen, trying to read the cursive writing, which swerved like a kid learning to ride a bike. Joseph Pierce was an engraver. His wife's name was Martha.

"No one can say this was made up?"

"Tampering with the census would be a federal crime," said George briskly. "And look, here are more articles about Joseph." He showed Evan the list, and clicked on one for Evan to read. The article said Joseph was described as "pigtail and all, the only Chinese in the Army of the Potomac."

"Pigtail!" Uncle Joe snorted at the description. "It was a queue. Anyone who wanted to return to China had to keep their queue."

"Anything else?" asked Evan. If one source was good, then two or more were even better.

"Here's a book from the National Park Services on Asians in the Civil War. A dot gov website is always a good bet," said George.

"Do you have the National Park book here?" asked Evan.

"I doubt it. We're a pretty small library. But I can do an interlibrary loan for you," said George. "That means the library borrows the book from another library. Might take a while, though."

"Is there anything I can have now?" asked Evan.

"Mmmm, here's an article. By Ruthanne Lum McCunn. It's seventeen pages long, and there's a twenty-cent-per-page fee to print."

"I don't have . . ." Evan started.

"Sold!" Uncle Joe interrupted. He reached into his wallet and pulled out a five-dollar bill.

"I can pay you back," offered Evan.

Uncle Joe made a face. "You're my nephew," he said. As if that explained everything.

George swiveled around and took the paper off the printer, even stapled them together. "Here you go," he said, handing Evan the paper. "And if you apply for a card, I can start working on that interlibrary loan."

Evan flipped through the packet. "There are no pictures!" he said, dismayed. That made George laugh.

"It's an academic paper," he explained. "Those tend to be heavy on words, not so big on pictures."

"It does talk about Joseph Pierce, though," said Evan, pleased. "That's good. And a bunch more people."

"You should say thank you, and you can just read a little bit at a time, no need to rush," said Uncle Joe to Evan.

Evan said thank you. George smiled at both of them. "You're a good uncle," he said. "You all should go to the meeting. You might have something to add, and anyway, you'd find it interesting, being history buffs."

"What do you say?" Uncle Joe asked Evan. "All the time I've lived here, I've never been to one of these, whaddyacallit, public meetings."

Evan didn't really want to go. The statue discussion did not seem like one he wanted to be part of. Especially since the discussion sounded confusing and angry. But Uncle Joe seemed interested, and Evan figured he owed him one after he paid for printing the article. "I suppose it couldn't hurt."

The meeting room was a large gray rectangle with no windows. At one end, three men and one woman sat at a long table, and the rest of the room was filled with people sitting, facing the table. All of the heads in the room turned and looked when they entered the room. One of the men at the table lifted his head. "Ah, this is a hearing on the Civil War statue in the town square," he said to Evan and Uncle Joe.

"We know," said Uncle Joe. He picked a seat up front and patted the chair next to him for Evan.

"Takes all kinds, I guess," said the man, who, according to the nameplate in front of him, was Councilman Thomas Byrne. What did that mean? George had said this was a public meeting, open to everyone.

"Forgive the interruption. Please continue," said the man sitting next to Thomas Byrne. His name was Councilman Harry Tate. He was speaking to a man standing at a podium. "You still have time." He gave Councilman Byrne a look. Evan guessed he didn't like Byrne's comment, either.

"I was pretty much finished," said the man. "I can't believe we're even having this discussion. My great-grandfather helped put up that statue, raised the money for it. The idea of taking it down is disgusting." Evan tried to get a better look at who was speaking, but the podium was angled toward the council members sitting at the table.

Councilman Tate smiled slightly. "If we weren't allowed to change anything in this town that was put up by your people, nothing would change around here. But times do change. And statues have gone down across the country, including Richmond, just as they once went up."

"People will forget their history," said the man, a young man, really, ending his statement. About half the room broke into applause as he started walking back to the seats.

Evan leaned over to Uncle Joe and whispered, "But sometimes we don't even know the whole history." Uncle Joe nodded and folded his arms.

The man from the podium heard Evan's comment. He turned toward Evan. "What'd you say?" he said roughly.

Councilman Tate knocked on the table. "All comments must be addressed to the chair," he said. "And such comments must be courteous in tone. Though the chair will recognize the young gentleman if he wishes to speak."

The young gentleman was *Evan*. He froze. Maybe if he didn't move, they'd forget he was in the room. This was not what he had signed up for when he said he'd go to the meeting.

Uncle Joe gave him a nudge. "Sure, tell 'em if you're inclined."

Evan stayed rooted to his chair. Public speaking was about as appealing as swimming with sharks. But he had something to say, didn't he? It's now or never, he told himself. Do it. Do it! He launched himself at the podium. Councilman Tate asked for his name. Evan told him.

"Are you a resident of this town?" asked Councilman Byrne.

"We moved here a few weeks ago," said Evan. He pointed at Uncle Joe. "That's my uncle. He's lived here a while." Uncle Joe nodded and sat up straighter.

Councilman Tate took over. "Now, Evan, did you have a comment for the council regarding the statue in the town square?" Mr. Tate smiled, as if to make up for Mr. Byrne's grumpiness.

Evan laid the article George had given him on the podium. He was starting to sweat. One of the pages stuck to his hand and he had to flap his hand to get it off. He pulled the microphone down toward his mouth, and it let out a high-pitched squeal. Not a good sign. Still, Evan stayed at the podium, grateful that his shaking knees weren't showing. He thought about what George had said about the statues going up around the same time, but the council members already knew that. It was time for a different argument.

"I was just saying that instead of worrying about forgetting history, and I don't think anyone around here is going to forget about the Civil War anytime soon, it's more important to know the whole history." He wiped his hand across his forehead. "I found out that there were Chinese soldiers in the Civil War, and even my teacher, Mrs. Norwood, didn't know that."

Councilman Byrne raised one eyebrow. "That's very interesting, son, but I don't know what that has to do with what we're talking about."

"Um . . . Son?" asked Evan.

"That's just an expression around here, which you'd know if you'd been living here more than fifteen minutes." Then he laughed in a not pleasant way.

Councilman Tate knocked on the table. "The council member will refrain from making comments during testimony."

"But that's the point," Evan blurted out. "Knowing that people looked like me, during the Civil War, that means something." He held up the article. "These are Chinese soldiers who fought in the Civil War. Joseph Pierce for starters. There are more." His words were staggering, tumbling out, threatening to fall at any moment. He took a deep breath. "But when you have a statue, it's like one idea about who fought in it is stuck in concrete."

Someone in the audience started to clap, and others joined

him. Some people booed. Councilman Tate knocked on the table, calling for order. In the middle of the clapping, there was a loud bang. The man who had spoken before Evan had walked out, slamming the door behind him. Evan sat back down.

"Hey," Uncle Joe whispered. "You did really well. I'm so proud of you!" Uncle Joe put his arm across the back of Evan's seat. That almost made getting up and talking in front of everyone worthwhile.

"I made that guy mad. And that one guy up there doesn't seem very friendly," Evan whispered back.

"You're never going to make everyone happy," said Uncle Joe. "It's more important to stand up for what you believe in." He took out his phone and wrote down something. "And I'm going to pay attention to the next time this guy runs for office." He meant Councilman Byrne.

Even when it was all over, though, Evan could not quell the shaky feeling inside of him, the sense that someone had struck a note inside him and now it was vibrating endlessly. It was that man's anger, the one who had slammed his way out of the room. This was why he hated his thing, his Mr. Sensitive, sometimes. In order to feel the lie, he felt other people's moods, keenly. In the chest. Why should he care? Why couldn't he just shake it off?

Going back outside helped. The sun hung low in the sky, keeping the late afternoon air warm, creating long shadows from the statue they had just been debating. Evan put his hand up to shield his face, to look at the statue. The sun was behind the statue, turning it dark and faceless.

"We should go get ice cream," said Uncle Joe. "To celebrate."

"Celebrate?"

"Heck yeah! You got up there and spoke up before the council. I couldn't do that." Uncle Joe twitched, like he was shaking off a bug. "Not without some serious reinforcements."

"Mom would probably be mad if I had ice cream before dinner," Evan pointed out. "The question is, if she'd be madder at you or me."

"Oh, me of course," said Uncle Joe. "I'm the adult. Well, maybe we can pick up some to take home. I think they have ice-cream pints over at Charlotte's." He pointed across the way to a sign with pink swirling script. BURGERS AND FRIES! MILKSHAKES!

Evan saw something else. Across the square, poking into a garbage can, was a medium-sized dog with thick, dark brown fur. A girl. She pulled out a balled-up sandwich wrapper, nosed it open, and ate the bit of sandwich inside. Then, she rose up on her hind legs again, stuck her head back inside, and pulled out a plastic cup with ice melting in the bottom, holding the top edge in her teeth. She set the cup on the sidewalk and took out an ice cube.

"Someone's having dinner," said Evan. They walked across the square to take a closer look.

"Doesn't have a collar," said Uncle Joe. "And seems to know her way around a garbage can."

"Maybe she's a stray," said Evan. Evan knelt down and called to the dog. She stared at him for a moment, then came over and smelled his outstretched hand. "Hey there." He ran his hand over her head. After a few more strokes, she moved closer to him. Her fur was soft. "She's nice." Now the horrible, buzzy feeling was going away. The dog calmed him.

"You better run before the dog catcher shows up," said Uncle Joe, teasing. He reached over and gave her a scratch behind the ears.

Evan petted the dog for a few more minutes. A plan was forming in his mind. "You know what's better than ice cream?" Evan asked his uncle.

"Pie?" asked Uncle Joe.

Evan gestured toward the dog, who was now smiling at him. Open mouth, sparkly eyes, a long pink tongue lolling out.

"Now wait a minute," said Uncle Joe. "One minute ago, you were telling me that I'll get in trouble with your mom if I give you ice cream, but now you're saying it's okay to bring home a stray dog?"

"Well, I have definitely gotten in trouble for eating before dinner, but technically, Mom has never said, 'don't bring home a stray dog.'" As if in agreement, the dog put her paw on Evan's foot, which made Evan feel more determined.

"Your mom will have my hide! Joe, why can't you be more responsible? Who's the adult here, Joe?" Uncle Joe raised his voice, pretending to be Evan's mom. "Not that she isn't a sweet pup."

Evan sensed an opening. "What if . . . the dog happened to, um, follow us?"

"Follow us?"

"As in, you didn't decide to bring her home, it just happened. She just . . . jumped in the truck."

"Well, that's another matter entirely," said Uncle Joe, stroking his beard. "Then it sounds like fate, and who are we to deny fate?"

"The question is, how do we make fate happen?" said Evan. He looked at the businesses around the square. "Can I have money for a hamburger?"

"That's not really fate," said Uncle Joe, smiling.

"You call it a hamburger," said Evan. "I call it fate."

CHAPTER NINE

CELESTE

Celeste was outside, sitting on the step when the truck pulled up. She'd been sitting outside because she felt like it, not because she had been hoping that someone might walk by and start a conversation. She had noticed that Ella from her world history class walked her dog around five o'clock. Ella was one of the more tolerable people at school, someone with something interesting to say.

Ella had not come by with her dog today, but now Evan was getting out of the truck with a dog. And a slightly guilty smile. He'd tied a rope around the dog's neck and was holding the other end. *Evan, what are you up to?*

Still, she couldn't help making a long *oooooh* sound as she made her way to the dog. This dog was cute, a word that Celeste tried to avoid, but it definitely applied here. The dog looked like she was smiling. Celeste held out her hand, so the dog could smell it, and then began petting her, gently at first and then working into a full-blown ear and neck rub. "Who's a good dog? Who is a very good dog?"

"Why are you talking like that?" asked Evan. "You sound like you're talking to a baby."

"That's how you're supposed to talk to dogs," said Celeste. "I read that somewhere." She returned to her higher-pitched voice. "So where'd this beautiful girl come from?"

"She, uh, just jumped in the truck," said Evan. Celeste stifled a laugh. As good as he was at sussing out other people's lies, Evan himself was a terrible liar.

"Uh-huh," said Celeste. "Just randomly jumped in, huh?"

"Maybe she was hungry," said Evan. Uncle Joe nudged him and laughed.

"Well, she's definitely used to people. Are you sure her owner wasn't around?" asked Celeste.

"No tags and she was eating out of a garbage can," said Evan.

"People drop their dogs off in the country when they can't

afford 'em," said Uncle Joe. "They don't want to take 'em to a shelter, so they just ditch them."

"That's terrible," said Celeste. She imagined how the dog felt after the car drove off, expecting the family to come back. Maybe even thinking they'd made a mistake. *How long would a dog wait?* she wondered.

"What's going on here?" asked Mom, stepping outside. She put her hands on her hips and looked at the dog. "A dog?!"

"She, um, followed us home," said Uncle Joe. "Just jumped in the truck. What could we do?"

"Uh-huh," said Mom. She wasn't falling for it any more than Celeste. But at the same time, she didn't say no, either. If anything, she seemed amused. Celeste continued her all-out petting assault. Mom stroked the dog on the head, exactly once, and then folded her arms.

"I think Mochi would be a nice name," said Evan. "Her coloring reminds me of the chocolate mochis back home." So typical of Evan, thinking of food, but it was a good name.

Celeste pulled out her phone. "I can order a nametag for her and put my phone number on it."

"It should be my phone number," argued Evan.

"Whoa, whoa, I don't know if we should name the dog. We

don't even know if we're going to keep her," said Mom. "A dog is a lot of work."

Somewhere in the distance, a car honked. Mochi opened her eyes and turned her head toward the sound, cocking her head.

"A guard dog!" said Evan. "You're always complaining about wanting the doors locked, but burglars avoid houses with dogs."

"That's true," said Mom slowly.

"You're also worried about us adjusting. Dogs promote mental health," said Celeste.

"Did I say that?" said Mom. "I retract that comment. My only concern is your academic performance." Mom's phone rang; she looked at it and then put the phone in her pocket without answering.

"Based on what I'm seeing, a dog is a lot of love," said Uncle Joe. Mom made a face at Uncle Joe. "You're supposed to be on my side!" she mock-scolded.

"Maybe I am on your side and you just don't know it yet," said Uncle Joe. *"Gǒu lái fú."*

Mom laughed. "I wish."

"What does that mean?" asked Evan.

Mom scolded him. "If you spoke more Chinese, you'd know!"

"A dog brings luck," said Uncle Joe. "Or fortune."

"That's before vet bills," said Mom.

"Let me get a picture of you guys," said Uncle Joe. Celeste and Evan sat on either side of Mochi, putting their arms around her. "Two kids and a dog. Can anything be more classic?" He showed Mom the picture.

Mom's face softened. "You guys are ganging up on me. And I guess it's up to me to decide, huh? Just me. The adult."

She was talking about Dad, Celeste realized. Mom had to make all the grown-up decisions alone, without Dad. She wondered if Mom missed Dad. She herself tried not to. *He's a jerk*, she reminded herself.

Evan stood up. "I'm going to get her a bowl of water," he said. Celeste stayed with Mochi. Mochi rolled over on her back.

"Here's the thing. Even more than the guard dog, I'm interested in this." Mom gestured toward Celeste and Mochi.

Celeste stopped, in the middle of a belly rub. "What."

"Well, up until about three seconds ago, you were smiling," said Mom. "I miss that smile."

"I'd feel better, knowing you had a dog," said Uncle Joe.

"I thought you said this was a safe town!" teased Mom.

"That's not what I meant," said Uncle Joe. "You need something besides just safety, and I think this dog might be it. Something just feels right now."

Mochi sat up and wagged her tail. Ella was walking down the street with her dog, a tiny black thing with a tuft of hair on its head. "Is that a new dog?" asked Ella, her voice rising with excitement.

"You want to meet her?" asked Celeste. She picked up the rope and met Ella halfway across the lawn.

Mochi clearly had once belonged to someone, though no one responded to the lost dog notices they put up around town. She brought her leash to them when she wanted to go for walks and banged on the water dish when it was empty. She knew how to play fetch. But mostly, she seemed so happy to be with them. She loved leaning against Evan while he played video games, or hanging out with Celeste while she did homework. After a few days, Celeste could not imagine coming home from school and not having Mochi there.

"You need to close the freezer door," Celeste told Evan after school one day. Evan got home before Celeste did and usually made a mess, making his snacks. It was a hot day, so he'd probably gone digging for a Popsicle.

"I didn't go into the freezer," said Evan.

"Sure you did! It's open, isn't it?" Celeste reached over and pushed the freezer drawer closed with her foot. It was one of the refrigerators with a freezer drawer on the bottom. The house was warm, but Mom didn't want to put the air-conditioning on yet.

"It might have been open, but I didn't do it," said Evan stubbornly. Evan was hot, too. His face was red and Celeste could see a bead of sweat roll down his temple.

Celeste rolled her eyes. Why argue about the obvious? "Whatever," she said. She and Ella were going to go for a walk with the dogs. It was a thing they'd started doing after school. Ella said it was one of her chores, so Celeste made walking Mochi one of her jobs, too.

Mochi pranced in and looked at them, tongue hanging out. "It's hot," said Evan. "Let me throw a few ice cubes in Mochi's water bowl."

Before Evan could move, though, Mochi grabbed the

handle of the freezer and slid it open. Then she jumped into the freezer, nestling herself among the bags of frozen vegetables. She let out a long sigh of contentment.

Celeste and Evan looked at each other, open-mouthed, for a moment, then burst out laughing.

"Mochi, no," said Celeste, trying to sound serious. "That's not what the freezer is for."

"She knows you don't mean it," said Evan. "Look at her. She's so proud of herself for finding a cool spot."

Mochi nosed around the freezer and helped herself to an ice cube, crunching noisily.

"That is one smart dog," said Ella later, on their walk, when Celeste told her about the freezer. Ella tugged on her dog's leash. "Kiki is still trying to figure out stairs, much less how to open doors."

"Now we have to figure out how to keep her from opening the freezer," said Celeste. She tried to sound like she was complaining, but the truth was, she was proud.

"You can put a lock on it," said Ella. "My aunt got a fridge lock when my cousin was little to keep her from opening the door."

"We should get one for Evan," said Celeste. "He's eating, constantly."

"He's probably going through a growth spurt," said Ella.

"Then he'll be taller than I am," said Celeste. She and Evan were nearly the same height, even though Celeste was older.

"A colossus," said Ella. She liked using unusual words. That was something Celeste appreciated about her.

"Brobdingnagian," said Celeste, matching Ella. "Picked that one up in English." They had been reading *Gulliver's Travels*.

"Isn't Luke Ellis in English with you? He's, like, obsessed with you," said Ella. "The other day he found this news article about some guy named Michael Pao from Schuyler who got arrested. He was wondering if he was your dad."

"Ugh, Luke," said Celeste lightly. Keep everything the same, she told herself. Don't change your voice, your step, your expression. "That's gross. Is googling me one of his hobbies? And just to be clear, unlike Haddington, there are tons of Asians in Schuyler and we're not all related just because we have the same name. Luke needs to catapult himself into the sun."

"He can go join the shoe guy," said Ella.

"The shoe guy?" asked Celeste.

"That guy, Michael Pao. He was in the news because he had swindled his friends in some kind of shoe scam, and they caught him," said Ella.

It was socks, not shoes, thought Celeste. Then she blinked back the tears that had sprung unexpectedly into her eyes. Then she realized the other part of what Ella had said. They had caught him.

Celeste waited until Mom had gone out grocery shopping to tell Evan about Dad. She showed him an article she had found online. It wasn't a big headline article. She had to look for it.

Evan stared at the screen numbly for a moment. "They arrested him," he said quietly.

"Yeah, of course they arrested him," said Celeste brusquely. She waited for Evan to agree but instead he lowered his head and began taking in big gulpy breaths. Slowly, Celeste realized what was happening. Evan had been holding out for another explanation.

"You were still hoping," said Celeste. She put her around him. "Hoping that there would be a different story about Dad."

"I'm so stupid," said Evan, burying his face into her shoulder. Celeste felt her sleeve become wet.

"You weren't stupid," said Celeste. Not *that* stupid, anyway, she thought. "You were hopeful."

"Feels like the same thing," said Evan. "Hoping was stupid. I just never, I never sensed that Dad was lying to us."

"To be fair, Dad never came to us outright and said, I am not going to cheat the neighbors, take everyone's money, and flee," said Celeste. "So there wasn't a lie to detect."

Mochi wedged herself between the two of them, and then leaned over and licked Evan's face worriedly. Evan smiled slightly. "It's okay, Mochi," he said.

"She's worried about you," said Celeste. "She's wondering what's happening."

"Don't you miss Dad sometimes?" asked Evan.

"I miss our old house, our old school. My friends, before they got mad at me," said Celeste. "Dad took that away from us when he left."

"Dad is the reason why we know about the Chinese soldiers," said Evan. "In a weird way."

"Under that theory, Dad is the reason why this boy at school thinks he is in love with me," said Celeste.

"Can't you be mad at someone and miss them?" asked Evan.

"It's easier just to be mad," said Celeste. But as soon as Evan named the feeling, she felt the same thing. She was mad at Dad, and wanted nothing more than for him to be around so she could tell him how mad she was.

CHAPTER TEN

MAX

When Evan had come back from the library with an article on Chinese soldiers in the Civil War, he became an instant celebrity. Even the principal stopped by to congratulate Evan. "This puts a new face on Battlefield Day," said Mr. Hawthorn, shaking Evan's hand. "Just goes to show there's always something new to learn."

"Yes, sir," said Evan. Max had taught him that. Saying *ma'am* and *sir* in Haddington got you a lot of good will.

"Maybe you'll go to the University of Virginia and study history," added Mrs. Norwood. That was her highest praise, to tell someone they might go to UVA. "In the meantime, I believe I'll call the *Haddington Clarion* to see if they might be interested in this story. Get some press for Battlefield Day."

"I guarantee they've never had a story like this," said Mr. Hawthorn on the way out of the room.

Max was happy for Evan. He was glad that Evan's story was true, and that Evan could be a soldier on Battlefield Day without anyone giving him a hard time. But then he'd remember his own silence when Brady had asked whether Evan's picture was real, and he felt guilty. Why hadn't he spoken up? Was it because he thought Brady might be right? It didn't matter, Max tried to tell himself, now that Evan had come back with proof.

It didn't take long for Brady to come up with a new reason to pick on Evan. Brady grudgingly accepted that the Chinese soldiers were real, but now they weren't good enough.

"They're Union soldiers," said Brady at recess. "Yankees."

"Some of them fought for the South," said Evan, which briefly stumped Brady.

"None of them are famous. Not like a general, or even a leader during an important battle," said Brady.

Max didn't wait to jump in this time. "Most people aren't famous. That's not what's important," said Max. "Brady, your family didn't have any famous people in the war."

"Famous for anything good, anyway," someone, maybe Taylor, murmured.

The kids around them let out a long *oooooo*. Brady's eyebrows went into a deep, angry V. "Jubal Griggs was renowned for his crack marksmanship," he said. "For being a soldier's soldier."

The group sighed, bored with Brady's comment. How many times had they heard that description?

"You think you're so great because you found a couple of Chinese soldiers," said Brady to Evan. "They're not even family."

"I know that," said Evan. "I'm just happy that there's someone who looks like me, that's all." Brady could not pierce Evan's happiness.

"They're famous to me," Evan told Max later. "All these men. Joseph Pierce and Thomas Sylvanus. Hong Neok Woo." They were spending Saturday afternoon wandering around town with Chessie and Mochi. Max had held the dogs while Evan went into Charlotte's and got milkshakes. They pressed their faces into the glass at Unik Geek, trying to look at the comic books.

"Which one was Thomas Sylvanus?" asked Max. Evan talked about the men he had read about the same way Max's mom talked about relatives in the past—in snippets and stories.

The stories were easy to remember, but it was harder to attach names to them.

"He was the one that had gotten captured by the Confederates, and a general asked him what it would take for him to switch sides. He said they'd have to make him a brigadier general," said Evan. "He made everyone laugh."

"And that other guy? Hong...?" Max couldn't quite remember the exact sounds.

"Hong Neok Woo," said Evan. "He signed up to fight, even though people told him not to. They told him it wasn't his fight and he signed up anyway because he wanted to end slavery."

"And then there were those guys who were the sons of the Siamese twins in the *Guinness World Records*," said Max. He had remembered the photograph, two Asian men in full suits, joined somewhere along the midsection.

"Yeah! They were on the Confederate side. Their dads owned slaves," said Evan. "North Carolina, I think."

"Never would have guessed it," said Max. He took a long pull on his straw, finishing the last of his strawberry milkshake. The cup made a hollow, rattling sound.

"Who is that guy, anyway?" asked Evan. He pointed to the statue in the middle of the square.

"I think he's just supposed to be a regular soldier," said Max. The two boys walked over for a closer look. The statue was a man with a thick mustache and wide-set eyes.

"You know, I've probably walked by this statue hundreds of times, and this is the first time I've really stopped to look at it," said Max. "He looks a little like my mom's brother. Especially during the quarantine, with the mustache and the longish hair."

"They're talking about taking it down," said Evan. "I went to a meeting about it with my uncle."

Max pretended to stagger back. "Seriously? You went to a council meeting? My dad has to go to those and says they're deadly boring." He threw his cup into a trash can. "Well, okay, now that you've been to the most boring thing in Haddington, I feel like you need to go somewhere fun," said Max. He clucked to Chessie. "Let's go."

They walked across town to the First Methodist Church of Haddington. Max jerked his thumb toward the cemetery. "My family's buried there, you know."

"This is the fun place you're taking me?" said Evan.

"No, it's on the far side. But, I mean, cemeteries are interesting, even if they're not fun. Looking at dates and stuff.

124

Seeing what people wrote on their tombstones. There's one with a recipe for biscuits," said Max.

"Have you tried it?" asked Evan.

"Tried what?"

"The recipe. It was probably some really good, secret recipe that the person didn't want to give up until they were dead," explained Evan.

"Maybe we can go by on the way home and get it," said Max. "But for now, ta-da!" They were standing next to a huge oak tree by the edge of a ravine. The Dalloway ravine.

Evan looked down into the ravine. "This is your idea of fun?" Mochi whined and pulled back on her lead, nudging Evan away from the edge.

"Not this. *This.*" Max reached up into the tree, and pulled out a thick, sawed-off branch tied to a rope. The other end of the rope went high up in the tree, tied to a branch that hung out over the ravine. "It's a swing. Watch."

Max made sure the rope wasn't caught on any branches, then went back as far as he could from the edge of the ravine before running back toward it at full speed. At the last second, he jumped, gripping the stick, smoothed by so many other hands, and swung out over the ravine. Chessie started barking.

This was the moment Max loved best, the moment of weightlessness, as close to flying like a bird that he'd ever come to. He liked feeling the wind against his skin, the feeling of being unattached. There was always part of him that wanted to let go of the rope, to see how far he would fly, but he never did. The swing went out into a wide horseshoe, and then returned him back to earth.

"That was amazing!" said Evan. His eyes lit up.

"Best ride on earth. As good as any ride at an amusement park, and no waiting in lines," said Max proudly. He held out the stick. "Now you try it."

"He's not allowed on the Dalloway swing," said a voice above them. Max looked up, shading his eyes. It was Brady and Alex.

"Of course he is," said Max.

Brady came huffing down the hill. "The Dalloway swing is only for people who belong to the church, or at least have kin there," he said. "You don't have kin in the church, unless you have some other surprise you found on the Internet. Maybe a surprise result on a DNA test."

"It's not a rule," Max tried to assure Evan, who took two steps backward, away from Brady, away from Max and Alex.

"Sure it is," said Brady. "Do you know anyone who went on the swing who *wasn't* with the church?" He turned to Alex. "Do you?" Alex shrugged.

"It's not like you go to church," said Max.

"I went when I was little," said Brady. "I've got kin here." He rocked back and forth on his feet, grinning. He was standing firmly in the take-off spot for the swing, feet planted wide, arms crossed. "Grandparents, great-grandparents, great-great-grandparents . . ."

"Move," said Evan, interrupting him.

"No," said Brady. "Now where was I? Great-great-*great*-grandparents. Not to mention aunts, uncles . . ."

Suddenly, Evan tossed the stick around Brady, leaped out, cat-like, and neatly grasped the stick on the other side mid-air. "Wahoo!" he shouted as he sailed into the air. The wind fanned his hair out. Evan grinned widely, waving as he flew over the ravine. He landed on the other side of the tree, dragging his feet in the dirt to come to a stop.

It was an impressive feat, but there would be a price to pay. Brady was on top of him as soon as Evan glided back to earth. "I told you that you weren't allowed to go," he said.

"You said it was some rule that sounded kind of fishy, if

you want to know the truth," said Evan. He pretended to look around. "Are the swing police coming?" Alex laughed, almost involuntarily.

Evan was standing dangerously close to the edge of the ravine. Brady would just need to bump him once, and Evan would go over. Max was about to call Evan over to him, to get him away from the edge, when Mochi inserted herself between Evan and Brady. Max held his breath. Brady took a step backward, and then leaned down and stroked Mochi once, on the head.

Brady gazed down at Evan. "You should be more careful. You don't seem to have a good idea of what the rules are around here."

"Oh, come on, Brady, you know that rule about the swing doesn't exist," said Max.

"Let's go," said Evan. "I got stuff to do." He turned away from Brady and began walking toward Max.

"We'll come back another day," said Max. That comment was as much for Brady as it was for Evan. He wanted Brady to know that he could not stop Evan.

"See you guys at school," said Alex, as if nothing had happened. Max shook his head and rolled his eyes.

Max and Evan walked a bit, until they were standing among the tombstones. They looked back toward the ravine. Alex was on the swing, alternating between screaming and laughing.

"Another turn would have been nice," said Evan.

"Do you want to go back?" asked Max.

"Now?" asked Evan. Max nodded. "What for? We can't swing."

"To fight them," said Max. They were both smaller than Brady and Alex, and he only scrapped with his brothers, but Max felt he had to make the offer.

"Since I like my face in its current arrangement, that will be a hard pass from me," said Evan dryly.

"You might have to, at some point," said Max. "Maybe you can train, get ready. We have a punching bag at my house."

"That's not a thing where I come from," said Evan.

Max didn't say anything, but spread out his hands to indicate the land, the grass, the hills. "But you're here now."

CHAPTER ELEVEN

EVAN

Brady usually came to class about one minute before the bell rang. Evan knew this because that was the moment his stomach tightened up, when he began to wonder if he was going to have a good day or not. When Mrs. Norwood called roll, it seemed official. Brady was not in school.

"Maybe he's sick," murmured Max.

"Maybe he fell into the ravine," said Evan. He regretted his mean thought, and then he didn't. It was Brady.

Evan wasn't the only one who seemed to notice Brady's absence. The whole mood seemed to lighten. When Mrs. Norwood wrote the daily math problem, she wrote a brainteaser instead of the usual problems.

Mr. Smith went outside during a rainstorm. There were no buildings nearby.

He did not have an umbrella and he wasn't wearing a hat.

His clothes were soaked, yet not a single hair on his head got wet.

How could this be?

"That's not a math problem!" complained Daniel.

"It's a thinking problem, nonetheless," said Mrs. Norwood. She allowed them to guess out loud. He was not in a simulator, nor was he inside a plastic cube. No one got it before it was time to go to music. Mrs. Norwood had arranged for the music teacher, Mr. Atkins, to teach a song from the Civil War called "Goober Peas."

"Does anyone know the name of the person who wrote this song?" asked Mr. Atkins cheerfully. Mr. Atkins could only come to the school twice a month to teach, but he always seemed to be in a good mood. Or maybe that's why he was in a good mood. When no one answered, Mr. Atkins told them. "The credited author is P. Nutt. That's what a goober pea is! A peanut!"

Mr. Atkins played the banjo, tinnily plucking along to the music while the class sang.

Sittin' by the roadside on a summer's day

Talkin' with my comrades to pass the time away

Lying in the shade underneath the trees

Goodness how delicious, eating goober peas

Think my song has lasted almost long enough

The subject is most interesting but rhymes are mighty rough

I wish this war was over, when free from rags and fleas

We'd kiss our wives and sweethearts and then we'd gobble goober peas

Normally Evan felt self-conscious about singing, but today he was free. Free to do as he liked. When it came to the last chorus, Evan tilted his head back and sang full-throated.

Peas, peas, peas, peas, eating goober peas

Goodness how delicious, eating goober peas

Peas, peas, peas, peas, eating goober peas

Goodness how delicious, eating goober peas!

Evan held the note for the last word and Mr. Atkins strummed a few extra notes. The class clapped and Evan took a deep bow.

"Wonderful enthusiasm," said Mr. Atkins, nodding his head. "Very good." Even though he was relatively young, Mr. Atkins was completely bald with a pink, shiny head.

"Wait," said Evan. "That's it! The man in the puzzle was bald. That's why his hair didn't get wet."

"You got it!" said Max, punching him on the shoulder. A few more kids reached over to high-five him.

Today, thought Evan, he was unstoppable.

On the way home from school, Evan and Max made up their own versions of the song. Evan couldn't remember the last time he had sung, just for the sake of singing.

"Fleas, fleas, fleas, fleas, oh my dog has fleas," sang Max.

"Poor Chessie," said Evan. "Get some flea medicine. And in the meantime, I'll make some cheese, cheese, cheese, cheese, macaroni cheese . . ."

"Tweeze, tweeze, tweeze, tweeze, my nose hair needs a tweeze!" Max pretended to yank a particularly stubborn nose hair. "My grandpa has pretty long nose hairs. And ear hairs. This song can be for him."

"Ds, Ds, Ds, Ds, earning grades of D," said Evan, serenading Max as he turned onto his street. "My mom will be vicious, if I bring home Ds!" Max turned and waved.

133

Evan hummed the rest of the way home. Maybe he'd call Uncle Joe and sing the song to him. Uncle Joe was on the road, heading down to South Carolina for work.

When he opened the door, the first thing he saw was glass, glittering in the sun.

Mochi's cries echoed off the walls, sharp with pain. She was limp-running around the house, favoring her front right paw. Evan dropped his backpack and softly caught her by the bathroom. "It's okay, Mochi. It's okay," he crooned. He examined her paw. A piece of glass glinted from the pad on her foot. Evan plucked it out with the tips of his fingers. Blood oozed out. Evan grabbed a towel to press down on the cut. Mochi yelped and tried to nip him. Evan released the pressure slightly. Mochi bent down and began to lick her paw.

"What happened, Mochi?" Where had the glass come from? Evan tried to imagine what she could have broken, what could have led to the glass on the ground. Mochi stopped crying, but she was still panting, distressed. He checked her over, trying to see if she was hurt anywhere else, but she seemed okay. Evan lay down next to her awkwardly, halfway between the bathroom and the hallway, feeling her chest rise and fall under his hand. What just happened? What just happened to this very good day?

"What's that picture say?" asked the tall officer, Officer McEnearney. He was looking at the big piece of artwork in the living room, eight horses painted in a flurry of brushstrokes. The two policemen seemed more interested in the house than the hole in the window, surrounded by spidery cracks.

"Eight galloping horses," said Mom.

Mom had rushed home when Evan called her, arriving just a few minutes after Celeste did. Celeste was the one who said that they should call the police. Mom had not wanted to call the police because no one was hurt. It wouldn't matter. Evan was confused at first—the police did not do medical emergencies for pets, did they? "No, dummy," said Celeste. "We should report this. Make a record." A record of what?

Celeste insisted. Now they had two officers in their living room, looking at their lives, and them, like curious visitors to a museum exhibit.

Officer Nelson was shorter and stouter than his partner. He

sniffed the air. "Smells like a Chinese restaurant in here. You cook? Can you make lo mein?"

"I cook a lot of things," said Mom. Maybe to someone who did not know her, Mom sounded matter-of-fact, but Evan knew enough to recognize she did not like his question.

"Maybe you can cook dinner for us," said Officer Nelson. Maybe he was trying to be friendly. But the officers were supposed to be helping them, not asking for dinner.

Officer Nelson stood up and peeked over the swinging doors into the kitchen. "Hey, John," he said. "They've got a rice cooker just like the one at Jade Palace in Belledale."

"What do you think happened here," said Celeste, drawing the officers' attention back to the window.

"Maybe a car came by and sent a rock through the window." Officer McEnearney scratched his head. "It'd have to be at just the right angle, but heck, I broke my storm door once while I was weed-whacking. Shattered it but the glass stayed in place."

"Safety glass," said Officer Nelson, nodding solemnly. "Good invention."

The glass in the living-room window had not stayed in place. Bits of glass had fallen on the carpet, from a hole that was chest-high on Evan. Mom had wanted to clean it up, but Celeste told her to wait. The police needed to see everything.

"We should be able to find a rock then," said Evan. As annoyed as he felt, he wanted to agree with them, find a reasonable explanation. They all hunted around on the floor for a rock, a small stone. Nothing.

"Maybe it was a bird," said Officer McEnearney.

"That's a bird with a mighty strong beak," said Celeste. She sounded doubtful.

"It happens," said Officer Nelson mildly. He tapped the glass. "This is older glass; it's thinner."

Officer Nelson stretched his back. "Is someone upset with you?" asked Officer Nelson.

Evan felt his stomach turn into a stone. "You mean, you think someone did this on purpose?" said Evan.

Officer Nelson put his hands out. "It's a possibility, but let's not get ahead of ourselves."

"We barely know any people to offend," said Mom. "We're new here."

"Ah," said the police officer. He wrote something in his long, thin notebook. "Doesn't know the neighbors." He tapped his pen on the pad. "You should try to be more friendly. Take the dog for walks."

"We do take her for walks," said Celeste. "With the neighbors. We just don't know everyone."

The officers put on gloves and took out their flashlights, running the light over the walls, looking for clues.

"Got something," announced Officer Nelson. There in the doorway that led from Evan's room to the kitchen, almost at the floor, was a small black dot that had not been there before. The officer took a photograph of it. The mood changed now. It wasn't a rock or a bird or a car. Those were innocent explanations.

It was a bullet.

A bullet that had burst through the glass, flown across the kitchen, and pushed itself into the wood, flattening into a circle. A bullet fired from a gun. Someone had picked up a gun and decided to fire it at their house.

"Let's get a trajectory." Officer McEnearney took out a piece of string and held one end against the bullet. Officer Nelson then took the string and walked it through the kitchen to the living-room window. From the angle of the string, it was clear the bullet had come in from high. Officer McEnearney lowered his head and squinted along the string. The two officers traded looks. They said they were going to walk around the neighborhood and talk to some of the neighbors.

"What do you see? What's happening?" asked Evan.

"We'll let you know once we find out more information. Let's not get ahead of ourselves," said Officer Nelson. That seemed to be a favorite phrase of his.

The officers returned with Brady and a man holding Brady by the back of the neck, who Evan guessed was Brady's dad. They had the same nose, the same twist of the lips. Brady was wriggling around like a fish on a hook.

Brady. Brady had done this. It wasn't an accident or some weird misunderstanding. This was on purpose. This was how much Brady hated him.

Evan looked at Brady and felt overcome by fury, at Brady. He wanted to punch Brady in the face, watch him react with shock and pain, see blood stream down his face. He wanted to feel the snap of flesh and bone under his knuckles. He wanted to make Brady sorry, *force* him to feel regret and agony. Evan had never wanted to hurt anyone, and now his own hands curled into fists.

"This is Randall Griggs," said Officer Nelson, introducing Brady's dad to Mom. The man nodded curtly. "He's one of your neighbors up the hill. This is his son, Brady."

Mr. Griggs was large, impatient. He was nearly lifting Brady off the ground. He gave Brady a shove forward. "Say it," he commanded.

Brady staggered forward. His face looked like it had been sunburned, and he kept his shoulders bunched up like his dad was still holding him by the neck. He was silent for a moment, then he turned and said, "I'm only saying it to her, not to him."

"You say it to whoever I tell you to," said his dad. He raised his hand like a club. Officer Nelson said *Randall*, like the way a parent would, and Brady's dad lowered his fist. Too bad.

"You know each other?" said Mom, looking from Evan to Brady. Her phone buzzed, but she ignored it.

"We're in the same class," Evan said. He tilted his head toward Brady. "He was out sick today."

"Say it," said Randall. "I'll not ask a third time."

Brady stared at the ground. "I'm the one who shot your house," he said. He kicked the ground. Evan felt another jolt run through him, though this one came with another, more familiar feeling. The double image, the edges not quite lining up.

Brady was lying.

He's probably wishing we'd been home, thought Evan.

"You have a gun?" asked Mom. "At your age?" She turned to the police officers, wide-eyed.

"It was a rifle," Brady clarified.

"It's not unheard of, ma'am," said Officer Nelson. "I had one at his age. Lots of people do around here. Legally, the parents own it, but everyone knows who it really belongs to. It's like the dog." He smiled tightly and nodded toward Mochi.

"You could have hit someone," said Evan. He couldn't even bring himself to say the word, the worst scenario. Killed. He waited to see Brady's reaction.

"No one was home," said Brady. He barely moved his mouth to say the words. He didn't care.

"My dog was home," said Evan. "She stepped in the glass and cut her paw." For the briefest second, Evan thought he saw Brady's hard mask drop. A moment of surprise.

"Why?" Mom asked. "Why did you do it?"

"It's a hate crime," said Celeste.

"Whoa, whoa," said Officer Nelson. "Let's not start throwing around terms like that. Everyone, calm down."

"Look, Randall," said Officer McEnearney. "Why don't you tell the folks what you're thinking."

"Well, first there's going to be a trip to the woodshed," said Mr. Griggs. "For one. No video games, which I hate, anyway. Grounded for the foreseeable future. Double chores. And a few more things I can think of." Evan's skull began to pound, more warning that words were not matching up. Maybe it was the trip to the woodshed. He didn't know what it meant, but it sounded scary.

"Yes, sir." Brady seemed to shrink under his father's words.

Evan realized that the police were wrapping up. They considered the issue managed. "Wait," said Evan. "That's it?" His voice rose up on the last word and cracked.

Officer McEnearney looked from Evan to Mom. "Who is in charge here? You or the kid?" he asked Mom.

"I am," said Mom, though she seemed to be trying to make herself smaller, pulling her arms toward herself, hunching her shoulders.

"But, there will be charges," said Mom uncertainly. "A situation like this needs something else."

Officer Nelson put his hands on his hips. "Well, I tell you what, Randall's punishment is way worse than what the courts would do."

Officer McEnearney nodded. "Especially because he's a first-time offender."

"For now," said Celeste under her breath.

Officer Nelson was writing out a report on top of a metal box. The pen made a hollow scratching noise. "Obviously, ma'am, we're very glad that no one was hurt. There would be a different set of charges to consider," said Officer McEnearney. He pointed at Evan. "Look, Brady and your son go to school together. The damages have been minimal, and we are talking about a minor here in any case. He's accepted responsibility. You can press charges if you want . . . but that's what you'll be known for. Do you really want that? You're new here. Maybe just let this take care of itself."

His meaning was clear; if Mom pressed charges, she would be the bad guy, not Brady. They'd be the family that came to town and caused trouble. Evan stared at Brady, trying to will something to happen, anything. Brady remained unmoved.

"I will note that Brady has been given a formal warning," said Officer Nelson.

"And, uh . . ." Officer McEnearney looked over at Mr. Griggs. He rolled his eyes and nodded. "Mr. Griggs can contribute toward the cost of replacement."

"Contribute?" said Evan. "Why not the whole repair? It's not like they can put a patch on the window."

"*Dìdi*," said Mom shortly. "*Bié shuō huà.*" The comment was intended as a low-key way of telling Evan to be quiet but it seemed to infuriate Officer Nelson.

"You will keep this conversation in English!" he barked at her. Mom shrank down. Blood thundered in Evan's ears.

"We're not the ones in trouble here," said Celeste indignantly.

"You will be if you don't listen," said Officer Nelson. "I don't need you all speaking some secret language."

"Let's all calm down," said Officer McEnearney. "She was probably just saying mom stuff. But just the same, let's all speak the same language." He grasped Brady by the shoulder. "You just remember that if something like this happens again, we're coming straight to you." Brady nodded.

Who would have to get hurt next time? Evan wanted to ask.

Officer Nelson tore off the top sheet of the paper and handed it to Evan's mom. "Here's your report, ma'am. You talk to your landlord about getting that glass repaired. Everything just works a whole lot better around here if you try to get along, okay?" He turned to Evan and Brady. "If you two boys are in the same class, you should try to get along, too."

"Let's not get ahead of ourselves," said Evan. He said it so blandly that Officer Nelson just looked at him and smiled, thinking that Evan was agreeing with him.

CHAPTER TWELVE

CELESTE

"He didn't even say he was sorry," said Celeste, later that night. The policemen, the Griggses, were probably at home, watching television, getting ready for bed. They were done. But Mom, Evan, and Celeste, they were left with the mess, a mess that made the very air itself seem rearranged. They had cleaned, but kept finding bits and pieces left behind. A fleck of glass in the carpet. A black scuff mark from a policeman's shoe on the kitchen floor.

"Why should he? He's not," said Mom.

Celeste looked out the living window at the Griggses' house up the hill. Bright rectangles of light outlined the windows of the house, one large window on the first floor glowed with the bluish light of a television, and two smaller windows upstairs occasionally showed a person in a room. She wondered which one was Brady's room, where he was when he had pointed the gun at their house.

"I wish Uncle Joe were here," she said.

"I called Uncle Joe and let him know what had happened," said Mom. "But I told him not to leave the job." She snapped a food container closed, putting away the dinner they had left mostly uneaten. "He's trying to finish up soon, though."

Evan changed into the shorts and T-shirt that he used as pajamas, and then went into the bathroom. After a few minutes, he came out, crossed the hallway, and stood in the doorway to his room.

"Going to bed?" asked Celeste.

"Yeah," said Evan heavily. "In a minute." He wasn't going in. Why would he want to? The bullet had landed right there, in the other door jamb. A slight change in time, angle, inches, height—who knows what could have happened?

Celeste went into her room and got her blanket, pillow, and a cat-shaped stuffie. "I don't want to sleep in my room," she announced. "Not tonight." She started making a bed on the floor of Mom's bedroom. When Mom didn't say anything, Evan got his pillow and bedspread, and also made a bed on the floor next to Celeste.

"It's like we're camping," Mom said, trying to lighten the mood. No one said why they were here, acting like little kids, sleeping in one parental nest. It felt safer this way. Mochi came in and looked at them, whined and pawed at the blanket, and then settled in the hallway.

Mom got ready for bed, stepping over them to get to her pajamas, using the bathroom one last time, and then stepping back over them to get to bed. Outside the wind blew, clattering a tree branch against a window. Mochi jumped up and barked.

"It's okay, Mochi," said Evan. He patted the space next to him. "Come here." Mochi sat uncertainly near Evan's feet, then lay down with a sigh.

Celeste let her shoulders sink into the floor. "I wish we were home," she said. Mom switched off the light. Now they were just voices in the dark.

"We are home," said Evan.

"I meant Schuyler," she said.

"Where people hate us for an entirely different reason,"

said Evan. Mochi lifted her head and whined, probably at something she heard outside, but it seemed like she was whining at Evan's comment.

"At least it's a reason," said Celeste, emphasizing the last word.

"He's never liked me. He doesn't know me and he never liked me," said Evan. He moved his pillow and then punched it down, trying to get it in the right shape.

CHAPTER THIRTEEN

MAX

Max overheard Dad telling Mom about a call. He said it was Evan's family.

"What's going on? A call from Evan's house? Is everyone okay?"

Dad shook his head slightly. "It's not great, but it could be worse. It appears that Brady fired a gun at your friend Evan's house. No one was home, and I think that was intentional on Brady's part. Broke a window. No other damage. He received a warning." Half the time, Dad talked as though he were filling out a report, checking boxes, making notations.

"Just a warning? He's not going to court or anything?"

Dad shook his head. "Judge Thompson doesn't really want to deal with anyone under thirteen. He says they just learn bad habits from the older kids when they come to court, go to juvenile detention. Says it's up to us to do the tough talk until then."

"But shooting at Evan's house is serious," said Max.

"It is serious," said Dad. "But if you had your choice between the court and Randall Griggs, who would you choose?" Max didn't answer. Mr. Griggs was the kind of dad you kept your distance from. "This seems to be the age where the Griggses go off track a bit. But usually they come back and straighten up."

"We're still waiting on Charlie," said Mama.

"I said usually," Dad said mildly. "I might call on Randall, see how things are going." Dad and Brady's dad were friends from a long time ago. They had gone to high school together. Now Dad was the police chief, and Brady's dad trained dogs. Sometimes, Brady's dad helped out on searches with one of his dogs, when someone had gone missing. "The officers made it pretty clear to Brady that he should keep his nose clean."

Dad picked up his phone and went into his office. Max studied him while he talked, making notes on a pad that he carried around with him. Why wasn't Dad taking this more seriously? He didn't even seem mad. He seemed madder when Max had left the garden hose running last summer and flooded the front yard. From his office, Dad let out a chuckle, laughing at whatever the person on the other end said. It wasn't even bothering him now.

But Max worried about it. He felt responsible. Maybe they should have fought Brady and Alex. Maybe that would have stopped Brady from taking the next step.

The next day at school, Max pulled Evan to one side before class started. "I heard what happened at your house," whispered Max. When Evan looked surprised, Max added, "My dad's the police chief, remember?"

"I came home to Mochi crying and bleeding from stepping in the glass," said Evan. "But then that wasn't even the worst thing. The worst thing is that the police just let Brady off. Said his dad would punish him worse than they could."

"I'm sorry," said Max. He struggled to find the right words. "This sucks."

"You apologized before Brady did," said Evan. "Ha."

"I would never have guessed," said Max. "Not about the apologizing, I mean. The other thing." He didn't want to say *shooting* again, not in front of Evan.

"Brady just hates me." Evan looked away.

"There's hate and then there's *hate*," said Max. "I just can't believe . . ." His voice trailed off.

"Celeste wants to move back to Schuyler."

"But," Max tried to think. "Your uncle is here."

"You don't have to convince me. I don't want to move."

"It doesn't feel right," said Max. "It feels like Brady is getting away with something."

Evan chewed on the metal part of the pencil, leaving tiny dents. "We were told, basically, that if we made a fuss, pressed charges, that's what we'd be known for, and not in a good way." Suddenly, Evan's face changed from its usual gentle expression into something hard. Eyes narrowed, mouth becoming a straight line. Max followed his gaze.

Brady.

Max watched Brady all morning, looking at the way he acted as though nothing had happened. It wasn't fair. It wasn't right. Max waited until Brady showed up to play flag football and they had chosen teams. Then he said, "Hey, Brady." He spoke with an edge in his voice, cutting through the din of the other voices.

Brady looked at Max. "What."

The other kids fell silent, sensing something was about to happen. "So what happened yesterday, with Evan's house?"

Brady turned his head away, not looking at Max while he spoke. "Evan told you, huh?"

"No," said Max. "I heard my dad talking about it. I don't even think Evan would have mentioned it if I hadn't asked him."

The other students were gathering now to see what was happening. They created a circle around Max and Brady.

"I can't believe you did that, Brady," said Max.

"No one was home," said Brady. "No one was home." He crossed his arms.

"You shot at Evan's house," said Max.

"A gun," said Sophia. "You fired a gun?"

"A rifle," said Alex. "Must have been."

"There's no reason to do that. It doesn't matter that no one was home," said Casey.

"My dog was home," Evan pointed out. "She stepped on a piece of glass." This piece of information, more than anything, changed the mood of the group. They went from confused to angry.

"You haven't exactly been nice to Evan," said Taylor. "But I never thought you'd do this."

154

"Is Brady going to court?" Julia covered her mouth. "Is he going to jail? What's he doing here?"

"No charges have been filed," said Max. He felt grown-up when he said that. "Brady got a warning. Since he didn't get in trouble there, he's not in trouble with the school."

"That doesn't seem right," said Taylor. All the heads swiveled and looked at Brady. "There should be a consequence."

"Like what?" asked Casey. This is the question that had stumped Max. "What can we do?"

"We could all tackle him during the game," said Jack. "That's what he was going to do to Evan."

"Since you said that out loud," said Casey, "that's not going to work."

"And it doesn't seem, I don't know, like the same thing," said Julia. "I feel like it can't just be some random thing."

"Maybe," said Max. "It's not about what we do to Brady." He spoke the words slowly, letting the idea take shape. "It's about what we don't do."

Looking back, Max realized that he should have discussed this idea with Evan first. It was his house, after all. His dog.

His life. But the silent treatment was such a perfect idea. He'd suddenly remembered reading about a boy growing up in Utah in the 1800s with three brothers, including a really smart one, nicknamed the Great Brain. Whenever the boys were bad, the parents would not spank them. Instead the parents would give them the silent treatment for days or even a week or two. The parents would not speak directly to the kid, and if the kid spoke to the parents, the parents would not respond. According to the book, it was sheer torture. The kids would beg for a spanking instead.

The silent treatment was perfect because it solved all their problems. They couldn't physically harm Brady without getting into trouble, and they didn't have to get their parents or Mrs. Norwood involved. It was the only punishment they were uniquely capable of carrying out.

But when he said the words out loud, *silent treatment*, it seemed even more terrible.

"For how long?" Sophia asked. "A day? A week? A month?" She found the answer. "Two weeks."

"That sounds about right," said Max. A day seemed too short, but a month too long. Two weeks for the hate it took to shoot at someone's window. Two weeks to say *enough is enough*. He saw a round of nods.

Brady looked up at him and mouthed a word. *Don't?* Max wasn't sure but it didn't matter. He looked away.

"We all have to agree," said Max, gesturing to the group. "That this is the right thing to do in order for it to be effective. Is there anyone not here?" Sophia said she'd go get Amanda and Emma, who liked to read during recess, leaning up against the wall near the teachers.

"And . . . no talking at all?" asked Daniel.

"What do we do if we have to talk to him, like if we're assigned in pairs?" asked Julia. They were already talking about Brady as if he wasn't among them, but he was still there, listening.

"Just say the words out loud, without saying them to him," said Max. "Like, for the science project, say, 'Use magnets to draw iron out of the cereal,' and don't look at him."

"What if it's an emergency?" asked Julia.

"Well, of course, if someone's going to get hurt, really hurt, then say something," said Max.

"You gonna let them do this to me?" Brady said to Alex.

Alex looked at some spot in the air and mumbled, "It's only two weeks." If Alex was in, then everyone was in, Max figured.

"That includes Battlefield Day," said Evan. From the way he said it, it wasn't clear if that was a good thing or a bad thing.

"So it does," said Max. Maybe more than anyone else, Max knew that Brady had been looking forward to Battlefield Day since he was little. Max tamped down the tiny bit of sadness he felt for Brady. Brady deserved it.

Maybe it was not on purpose, but now the group was retreating from Brady. He was like the magnet from the science experiment they had on polarity, repelling all the metal filings.

"Is there anyone opposed?" asked Max. "Is anyone opposed to the silent treatment for Brady." The group stayed quiet. It was like they were doing it already.

"Raise your hand if you agree not to speak to Brady for two weeks," said Max.

Everyone raised their hand.

"I don't care," Brady said. "I don't care about your stupid silent treatment." He started to walk away and then stopped. Walking away was the point.

"Two weeks," said Max, making sure his voice was a calm counterpoint to Brady's rage. "The silent treatment starts now."

Brady turned and faced the crowd. "Hey! If you're a moron, don't say anything!" He flipped his hands in the air and laughed awkwardly. The kids looked at him silently. "I guess you're all morons! This is great!" He tried again. "Hey, who here is a quiet sheep?" He paused. "You're all quiet sheep, whaddya know!"

"He's going to say something to Mrs. Norwood," said Julia.

"No, he's not," said Max. "He won't want to seem like a whiner."

Mrs. Norwood whistled, signaling the end of recess. The group broke up and with that, people began talking again, in little dribs and drabs, as though a spell had been broken. Evan and Max made their way back up the hill toward the school.

Max watched Brady run from one group of kids to another, trying to get a reaction out of any of them, sticking his tongue out, jumping up and down wildly, shouting nonsense words. It was almost embarrassing.

"I probably should have cleared this with you first," Max

said to Evan. "Honestly, I didn't know what I was going to say until I said it."

"I mean, it's fine," said Evan. He stopped and looked up at the sky. "What if . . ." He stopped speaking because Brady had loomed up behind him, breathing so heavily that Max could see the hair on Evan's head moving. He was daring them to say something. Max resisted the urge to shove Brady back. Evan moved ahead without saying anything more. He was already ignoring Brady.

CHAPTER FOURTEEN

EVAN

Brady tried a few more times to get people to talk to him. Well, not talk to him, just acknowledge him, really. But even that didn't work. During lunch one day, he tried draping a slice of ham across his face, but that just got him in trouble with the lunch room monitor. When he tried to interfere with a game of Horse at recess, the other kids just set the basketball on the blacktop and walked away.

Brady settled into his new role. He was like a statue, silent but present. Expressionless. Just like the statue in town, sometimes the conversation was about him, even if it didn't include him. Yesterday, Mrs. Norwood had passed out copies of the weekly newspaper to use as a model for a Battlefield Day paper they were working on. "Look!" Evan pointed at the police report section of the *Haddington Clarion*. "Three reports of 'excessive engine noise,' all in one day. We know who that is." He glanced over at Brady. Runs in the family, he thought. Brady didn't respond, of course, but his ears began to glow red.

"Yeah, Charlie was driving all over town last Saturday night," said Max. "My dad was pretty annoyed."

Were all the Griggses like this, Evan wondered. Like, the Griggses throughout history. When he got home, he looked it up on the old laptop that Mom had set up for homework. It wasn't hard to find him; Jubal Griggs was a very unique name. Evan clicked on a link for a Civil War website. A page full of handwritten names and information popped up.

Jubal Griggs was halfway down the page, in spidery old cursive, though Evan found that if he hovered the cursor over a name, regular text would pop up, translating the handwriting. Evan scrolled across the page, looking at the information. Dates. Haddington, Virginia. Then, a few columns over from Jubal's name, very clearly, was the word *desertion*.

The great Jubal Griggs had abandoned his position, left his comrades behind. Some "soldier's soldier." This was the person that Brady worshipped, made such a big deal of. Evan laughed to himself as he printed out the page and highlighted the word *desertion* in bright yellow. It was time to turn the tables on Brady. The next day at school, he folded up the paper and slipped it into Brady's lunch bag.

Evan watched Brady out of the corner of his eye as Brady ate alone at lunch. Technically, he was not alone because there were not enough tables to make that happen. But he was alone, in the most absolute sense of the world. As the rest of the table chatted around him, Brady sat silent and hunched over, eating slowly. He was tearing off bits of his sandwich and chewing each bite carefully.

Evan felt a pang of recognition. He knew about making your lunch last. After the news got out that his dad had left town with the money of his friends and neighbors, he'd gotten his own kind of silent treatment at school. The other kids didn't shun him, exactly, so much as not include him in any conversation worth having. He stopped being included in birthday parties or afterschool playdates, and pretty soon it just got easier to stop talking. Taking a long time to eat your lunch gave you something to do, so you weren't just sitting there.

Brady reached into his lunch bag, and found the folded-up piece of paper. For a second, Brady's face lit up. He was so excited that for a second, Evan wondered if someone else had left a piece of paper in Brady's lunch bag. As Brady looked at the paper more intently, though, his face dimmed.

I know you, thought Evan grimly. I know who you come from. You come from bad people.

Brady looked frightened. He hurriedly refolded the paper and stuck it back in the bag. A wave of guilt washed over Evan. Maybe he'd gone too far. No, he told himself. This was nothing compared to what Brady did. This was no time to be Mr. Sensitive. What did Brady's brother's car say? NO MERCY. Evan twisted his feelings shut, turning them off like a leaky faucet.

When Uncle Joe got back into town, his first question was, "Have you taken care of that kid?" For a second, Evan thought that Uncle Joe meant the caring kind of "take care of." Of course, he meant the other, tougher kind.

"We've given him the silent treatment at school," Evan explained.

Uncle Joe considered Evan's statement. "I have friends

whose spouses sometimes do that. But for kids, I say, have it out. Fight. Blow off some steam."

"That's barbaric," said Celeste.

"It's the truth! It's just the nature of man," said Uncle Joe. When Celeste scowled at him, he amended his statement. "Human man." Evan wondered if Uncle Joe was disappointed in him, if he had fallen in Uncle Joe's eyes because he wouldn't fight.

Mom and Celeste had had their own, different reactions to the silent treatment. Mom had nodded and said, "Good," and went back trying to keep everything completely clean and neat, putting her energy into folding every towel into sharp-edged rectangles or scrubbing the sink until it gleamed. Celeste said she liked the silent treatment, and then added her own spin. Every morning she stood in the middle of the living room, looked toward the Griggses' house, and gave them the middle finger with each hand before going to school.

Now Uncle Joe was less than satisfied with Evan's answer. "Maybe I should go over there," he said, nodding toward Brady's house.

"They have guns, Joe," said Mom.

Uncle Joe tensed. "So do I."

"No, you don't," said Evan. He had not meant to speak. The words had just popped out, but the truth was obvious.

Uncle crossed his arms. "Fine. I could get a gun if I wanted one," said Uncle Joe. "I have friends."

"And then what," exclaimed Celeste. "Would you use it?"

"Let's not escalate," said Mom. "The window has been fixed. The boy is facing consequences. There's no need." Evan felt a twinge. Mom didn't mean what she was saying. He could hear it in her tone. Maybe she wanted Uncle Joe to escalate, but she was afraid.

"I just don't want them to think they have something over us," said Uncle Joe. He didn't talk any more about going over to the Griggses' house, but the go-along-to-get-along version of Uncle Joe seemed to be gone. Uncle Joe had changed.

Mochi had not been the same since that day, either. She was whinier, more high strung. Loud noises, like the clatter of a dish or even the slam of the microwave door, made her jump. Yesterday, Evan had accidentally dropped the toilet lid instead of setting it down gently and Mochi bolted across the house, hiding under the kitchen table. Evan had to crawl under the table and calm her down, whispering *it's okay, it's okay*, feeling her tremble under his hand. What did Mochi think had happened? Would she ever be okay?

Mrs. Norwood's students all received a worksheet to fill out with information they would use to make their character for Battlefield Day. Name, occupation, age, family, where they lived. It could be based on a real person or one you made up. There was even a place to draw a picture. The key, according to Max, was to have lots of details. The more elaborate you made it, the better Mrs. Norwood liked it. Don't say Confederate or Union for a soldier if you could say Army of Northern Virginia or Army of the Potomac instead. When they had started on the profiles, Julia raised her hand and asked, Had anyone ever put *slaveowner* on their profile?

Mrs. Norwood turned two deeper shades of red. "I mean, I suppose, they didn't say it outright, but based on the profile, you would think so," she stammered.

"We're pretending to be people from the Civil War," said Julia. "And people fought for the right to own other people, to enslave them."

"They did," admitted Mrs. Norwood. "But let's not get into

that. I don't want anyone to feel bad if their family actually owned slaves."

"Imagine how the people whose families were actually enslaved felt," muttered Taylor.

Julia was not the type of person to argue with a teacher, but this time she crossed her arms. "A person can't help their past," she said softly. "That's what my mom says. Our job is to learn from it." She didn't look directly at Mrs. Norwood when she spoke.

Mrs. Norwood put her hands up, in surrender. "I'm retiring, boys and girls. This is my last year running Battlefield Day. You can do with it what you like. Maybe it needs a new direction."

Evan thought about this conversation as he pulled his profile out of his desk, which unlike many of his other papers, he kept clean and unfolded inside a notebook. There was the way Julia talked about slavery that made it more personal, more human. You might be able to gloss over the word *slavery*, but to say a person wanted to own other people, to dominate everything about them and their lives and think of them as less than completely human, that reminded you that real people were involved. People who were moms and dads and kids, and who had birthdays and got mad over stupid stuff and had favorite foods.

Evan wanted to do the same thing with his words, but with a Chinese soldier, bring him to life. He had picked a soldier named Edward Day Cohota as the subject of his profile. A real Chinese person, who fought for the United States. Before the silent treatment, Evan wondered if he should pick a Union soldier, whether Brady would give him a hard time. Now he did not have to worry.

When Mrs. Norwood asked for volunteers to share a profile, Evan shot his hand in the air. He held up a photograph he had found.

"Edward Day Cohota had been brought to the United States from China by a ship captain and raised by the captain's family. He was part of the Massachusetts infantry. Some say he volunteered when he was eighteen; others said he was only fifteen," said Evan. He liked that Edward might have been so young; that he was only three years older than he was.

Alex raised his hand. "Isn't that the same story you told us about Joseph Pierce?"

"It happened more than once," said Evan. "The United States traded with China so there were American ship captains

169

there." When Alex looked skeptical, Evan showed Alex the picture of Edward Day Cohota that he'd found. A trim man in a suit, with a mustache. "This is from a government website. This isn't made up." Alex nodded, satisfied.

Evan described some of the battles Edward had been in. "Edward had fought in the Battle of Drewry's Bluff in Richmond and came out with seven bullet holes in his clothes, but he wasn't hurt. At another battle, a bullet came so close to his head that it parted his hair. Permanently." Evan took his index finger and ran it through his own hair, demonstrating. "At the Battle of Cold Harbor, he saved the life of a friend by hiding him under a rock during battle until he could take him to the ambulance station."

"See, class? These are good details," remarked Mrs. Norwood.

Evan finished his profile. "Edward reenlisted after the war and served in the army for thirty years. But because of another law that passed later, the Chinese Exclusion Act, Chinese were not allowed to become citizens, not even someone who had fought in the war. But when he was old and in a home for veterans, Edward still went out and saluted the flag every evening." Evan still did not say the other part he had thought about; how much Edward must have loved the United

States when it did not seem to love him back, would not call him a citizen.

Jack raised his hand. "If he was allowed to live here, why does it matter if he wasn't a citizen?"

Evan thought about it. "Would you like it if you were allowed to live here but not be a citizen?" he asked. "You can't vote, and maybe you don't know when someone is going to say you have to leave."

"No," said Jack quickly. He squeezed his arms against his body, as if trying to erase the fact that he had raised his hand.

"It's a really good story about his life," said Taylor. "I mean, it's sad, but it's good. I wish I had a story like that."

"A month ago, I didn't think I had a story at all," said Evan. He stopped. "It's your story, too, though. Edward's story belongs to you, not just me." Some stories made you change your mind about yourself and other stories made you think differently about others, but what was important was that it changed something about you.

Mrs. Norwood pulled him aside before lunch and said she knew someone who had studied the Battle of Cold Harbor, and maybe they would have more information for Evan. She also told him that she'd been to Cold Harbor. "It's not cold there, and it's not a harbor!" she said, laughing. Evan guessed it was the kind of joke that people who liked the Civil War told one another. It was better than being asked to be a scribe, that was for sure. He got an A on his spelling test. The cafeteria had chocolate milk for sale.

When Evan got home from school, Mochi was waiting for him, tail wagging. Maybe she was starting to feel better. Mom had left a blue cloth coat for Battlefield Day draped over the couch, with a note saying she was going to get some gold buttons for it. Evan tried it on—it was a little large, but it would work. Too big was better than too small.

"What do you think, Moch?" he asked. Mochi looked up at him and smiled just before Celeste flew in the door. "He sent a letter," said Celeste. She didn't sound like her usual confident self. Her voice was shaking, angry.

For a moment, Evan thought she was talking about the boy from school. But then he saw the name in the upper left-hand corner. Michael Pao.

"Dad wrote to us?" His heart leapt. Both of their names were on the envelope, but the letter had gone to their old house in Schuyler first, and was then forwarded to Haddington. "He doesn't know that we moved."

"There's a lot he doesn't know," said Celeste.

"What does it say?" asked Evan. The letter could say anything. *I love you. I miss you. This has all been a mistake.*

"You have to open it," said Celeste. She walked over to the kitchen drawer and took out a butter knife. "Open it."

Dear Celeste and Evan,

How are you doing? I miss you and think of you all the time. How is school going? Celeste, I wonder how your cello playing is coming along. Evan, are you still on time, on point, and on to the next thing?

Please take note of my new address. I hope you will write back soon, or even better, visit. It is not too long of a drive, though your mother has not been answering my calls. Is her phone number still working? Please ask her to get in touch with me.

I am spending my days trying to exercise and keep my mind at peace. I would like to tell you more, but my attorney has instructed me not to say more until my case is resolved. Let me say that I never intended for things to go this far.

Love,

Dad

173

Evan read the letter several times, trying to memorize every-thing in it. Then Celeste snatched the letter out of his hand.

"This letter . . . is . . . psychotic!" shrieked Celeste. She held the paper in front of her, screaming her reply. "How's my cello playing? Dear Dad, I gave up my cello because no one wanted to play with me. Dear Dad, We sold my cello when we moved across the country because there wasn't room for it in the car." She crumpled the paper into a ball and threw it across the room.

"Don't do that! It's my letter, too!" said Evan. He picked up the paper and smoothed it out. "He misses us," he said.

"He's using us to get in touch with Mom," said Celeste. "That's what's happening. He probably wants something, like money."

"We're his family," said Evan. "That's why he wrote."

"We're the people he left behind," said Celeste icily. "Read the letter, Evan. Think of all the things he could have writ-ten, but didn't. He makes it sound like he's writing to us from a business trip." She took a deep breath and let out a noise, a cross between a groan and a roar. "It's all about him. Count all the times he said *me*. Me me me." Celeste looked disgusted.

Evan had not read the letter the same way as Celeste. In the letter, he heard his father's voice. *On time, on point, and on to the next thing!* He had not forgotten. He ran his fingers over the letter. Dad had touched the same paper. *I never intended for things to go this far.* What did that mean?

"Don't go soft," Celeste warned. "I can tell from your face that your feelings-o-meter is going through the roof."

"He's our dad," said Evan.

"Dads aren't supposed to do what he did," said Celeste.

"Everyone makes mistakes." As soon as he said the words, a thought popped into his head. Did that include Brady? He squashed that thought.

"What am I supposed to do with that? Have a big ol' hug-fest?" said Celeste. She shook her head. "No way, uh-uh." She ran her fingers over her head. "It's easier to be mad."

It was easier. Safer. But it didn't feel, what was the word? Complete? "Maybe," said Evan. He tried to get his heart to slow down, his feelings to stop tangling and fighting with each other. Calm down. Instinctively, he reached his hand out. "Celeste, where's Mochi?"

As best as they could figure, when Celeste had come home screaming, Mochi had run for the back door and scrabbled it open. Uncle Joe had fixed the door with a lever-style door-knob. It wouldn't be hard for Mochi to pull down on it and swing it open. A dog who could open the freezer door could do that.

Evan and Celeste walked around the neighborhood, calling for her, and then when Mom came home, they drove around in the car, widening their search. Celeste made posters of Mochi and stuck them to lampposts. Every time they turned a corner, Evan's heart leapt, thinking he would spot Mochi at any moment. But she did not appear.

"Do you think she knows the way back home?" asked Evan. "How far could she have gone?"

"It says on this website that most dogs are found within two miles of home," said Celeste.

"I've heard amazing stories of dogs finding their way home," said Mom. She reached back to Evan and patted him on the knee while keeping the other hand on the steering wheel.

"But those dogs know that home is home," said Evan. How long did it take for a dog to know their home? "And she's been so jittery lately."

"I've called the vet, and joined some neighborhood groups online to leave pictures of Mochi," announced Celeste. "And

I'll hand out some more flyers at school. Someone must have seen her. You can do the same thing, Evan."

"Yeah." Evan leaned his face against the car window. "I will." He paused. "Sometimes it's hard to find the way home."

Mom caught his meaning. They had told her about the letter. "Some people don't deserve to call a place home."

"I wish he hadn't written," said Celeste. "And I won't write back. It's too hard." She leaned her head on Mom's shoulder. They were united.

Evan felt weary. Not in the physical way, even though they had walked around the neighborhood for an hour, looking for Mochi. His heart felt tired and worn out from worrying and wondering. Maybe Mom was right. Maybe Celeste was right. It was too complicated to hold all of these feelings inside. And who else did he have in the world?

"I don't care," said Evan. Now he was part of a united front. Safety in numbers. Almost immediately, though, he felt like he'd been punched in the head. He was lying, he knew that. He just hoped that particular lie, that he did not care, might become true.

CHAPTER FIFTEEN

JULIA

When Evan handed her the flyer, Julia had been thinking of her Battlefield Day profile, not dogs, and she half expected the piece of paper to have an old-timey photo on it, like hers. But instead, a bright-eyed, brown dog looked back at her with the word *LOST* over her head. Julia blinked hard and looked again.

She had seen that dog, or a dog that looked quite a bit like it, running down the street yesterday. She had been sitting at her desk, where she could see out into the front yard and the street, wishing she had more interesting homework to do. This was not a wish she could share with her friends, not even Taylor, because it would be too weird, too nerdy, too teacher's pet-ish.

"I saw a dog like this, running down my street, running at a pretty good clip." The picture was of the dog, from the front.

178

Mochi. Julia had seen the dog in profile. But still. The color was right. "Does she have kind of a curly tail?"

Evan nodded. "Yup, it makes almost a complete circle. I bet that was Mochi. Where was she headed?"

"You know Miller's field?" Evan shook his head, so Julia pointed. "I live on the other side of the school, on Water Street, over the bridge. If you walk down Water Street away from town, and turn left when you get to the old fire station. Go up the hill and you'll get to Miller's field."

Evan let out a huge sigh of relief. "This is really good. I'd been hoping someone would have seen her. Thanks a lot." Evan sounded very matter-of-fact, but Julia could have sworn she saw his eyes watering. She wasn't sure if she was supposed to say anything or not, but before she could decide, Evan went on to the next cluster of desks. Julia showed Taylor the flyer when she came in.

"My mom says that can happen with new dogs," said Taylor. "You have to be extra careful with them until they get used to the new house. Did Evan say what happened?"

"Just that she got out," said Julia. "But here's the thing I just remembered." She lowered her voice. "I also saw Brady out walking later that day, same direction."

179

Taylor made a noise. "Brady's always out walking. I would, too, if my big brother was Charlie Griggs."

"Yeah, but he also lives close to Evan, remember? It wouldn't be hard to go over and open the door." She pantomimed opening a door.

"Why would he do that?" asked Taylor.

"Why would he shoot at Evan's house?" responded Julia. "And he knows about dogs. His dad trains them." It was an exciting, if unproven, theory.

"We could ask Brady," said Taylor. "Except for the silent treatment. Darn." She giggled. Taylor didn't normally go out of her way to talk to Brady, anyway.

Julia had mixed feelings about Brady. Once he had shared a sandwich with her on a field trip when she had forgotten her lunch. But then a few days later he teased her for crying over a bad grade in math, which made her feel worse—both for the grade and the crying. She did think the silent treatment was fair, though she would have made it shorter, personally.

"Would he even tell the truth?" she asked. "If we asked him?"

"Good question," said Taylor.

"What are you guys talking about?" asked Sophia. Sophia was not Julia's best-best friend; that honor belonged to Taylor.

But she was certainly a close friend. Julia told her, and then focused on her presentation.

"My name is Sarah Rosetta Wakeman," Julia said. "I served as a Union soldier under the name of Lyons Wakeman."

The class collectively sat up, which was the reaction that Julia had hoped for. Not even Taylor knew she was doing this. After Evan's discovery of the Chinese soldiers, Julia had begun to wonder if there were other stories she didn't know about. Her aunt was in the navy. Were there any women who fought in the Civil War? After some digging around and a phone call to the library, she had her answer: Hundreds of women had fought in the Civil War. Lots of them didn't have to wear hot stuffy dresses.

"Sarah was from a really poor family, and the best way she could make money was disguised as a man. At first, she was working on a boat, but then she enlisted because she got a chunk of money for joining the army. She went down with her regiment to Louisiana, where she got sick and died, and was buried as Lyons Wakeman." The picture that Julia found showed a serious, smooth-faced soldier.

She had chosen Sarah's story because there was a photo, and because her grandmother's name was Sarah and her own middle name was Rose. It seemed like a sign.

Brady put his hand up for a moment, then sighed loudly and put it back down. *He probably wants to say that women weren't good soldiers,* she thought. But Sarah had survived marching hundreds of miles with bad food and water. She was tough; she lived when other soldiers had died.

"How did she pass herself off as a man?" Taylor wanted to know.

"They didn't check," said Julia, making air quotes in the air and drawing giggles from the class. She had wondered the same thing. "She wore bulky clothes, and pretended she couldn't grow a beard because she, or he, wasn't old enough yet."

"What would have happened if someone had found out she was a woman?" Sophia wanted to know.

"They would have sent her home," said Julia.

"Even if she was doing a good job?"

"I think so?" She looked to Mrs. Norwood for help.

"That's the way it was in those days. Women were not supposed to fight," said Mrs. Norwood. "Though there were women who acted as spies, which is another way of fighting, if you think about it."

"If she was buried as a man, how did people find out she was a woman?" asked Taylor.

"A family member found the letters she wrote home in the attic. Her family knew she was fighting as a man and they were okay with it," said Julia. "If it weren't for the letters, maybe no one would have ever found out."

Julia's head was so full of thoughts after her presentation, that she'd forgotten about her conversation with Taylor until lunch. "Did you hear?" asked Gabby. "Evan's dog is missing, and everyone thinks Brady took her."

"Everyone?" Julia felt excited. "Did someone see Mochi and Brady together?"

"I don't know who saw what," said Gabby. "I just know that everyone is saying Brady did it."

"I saw Mochi, and then I saw Brady a bit later," Julia explained.

"Makes sense," said Gabby, as if that confirmed the story. Julia wasn't sure. Did that mean Brady took Mochi?

"I was just wondering if there was someone else who saw that. Over by Miller's field."

"He was probably sneaking around," said Gabby. "So no one would see him. You know he knows how to train dogs, like his dad. Some of the kids are saying we should just give Brady a longer silent treatment. Like permanent silent treatment."

Permanent silent treatment? What did that even mean? Until the end of the year? Until they graduated from high school? For the rest of their lives? Julia wasn't sure. Then she thought about Evan, and how excited he was when Julia said she had seen Mochi. If Brady knew where Mochi was, then he should bring her back. That was more important than silent treatment, Julia decided.

Julia raised her hand and asked if she could get a piece of paper and a pen from the classroom. Usually the lunchroom monitor would refuse such requests, but Julia had a reputation. A good one. Mrs. Lentz gave her a quick nod and told her she could go.

During recess, Julia sat by herself, up on the hill overlooking where they usually played baseball or flag football. Carefully, thoughtfully, she wrote a note to Brady, and when they returned to class, she slid it into his desk when no one was looking.

CHAPTER SIXTEEN

BRADY

Brady found the note, folded twice, as he was looking for his worksheet on prepositions. A preposition, Mrs. Norwood had explained, expressed a relationship between a noun and another word or element. The car *on* the road. She arrived *after* the bell rang. For the last several days, Brady had been feeling as though there was no *anything* between himself and anyone else. The class had cut him off, left him alone.

It's fine, he had told himself. I don't need them. But in truth, when he spotted the note with his name on it, he wanted to cry with relief. The last few days had been miserable. Even when someone had left that note about Jubal Griggs, it was terrible, but at least it was something. This note was a tiny lifeline of communication. Someone was saying, I see you.

He waited until he got home—he wanted to run home but he wasn't going to give anyone the satisfaction of seeing him do anything different—past Charlie's closed bedroom door, up to his room, and on the bed. Nero, his dog, followed him.

"Wait a minute, boy," Brady told him, stroking his black, silky ears. Brady normally gave him a snack after school. It was their routine. His dad worked with dogs all the time, but Nero was one who had stayed, had become a pet. His dad said Nero had a keen nose but no stamina. He wouldn't stay motivated, wasn't pulling at the leash to get to the next task. "He's a Griggs for sure," his dad had said. "Too lazy for his own good."

Brady hated it when his dad said things like that, brushing them all in the same paint with his words. Like his name decided everything—who he was going to be, what he was capable of becoming. The only part he liked was that he was good at working with dogs, like his dad. He'd already helped his dad train a few dogs when they were pups—early skills, like housebreaking and basic commands.

He read the note.

Brady,

Evan's dog is missing. Many people in the class believe you did it. You have the means and the motive, and you were seen walking down the same street as her.

If you are responsible, you should bring her back. If you are responsible and do not bring the dog back, the class is consider-ing <u>permanent silent treatment</u>. If you are not responsible, please provide proof.

Brady read the note a few times and set it down. He didn't know what he had been expecting, but it wasn't this. Whoever sent the note didn't sign it, but Brady guessed it was a girl. The handwriting was neat and clear, written with a light blue pen. Brady tried to remember who he had seen with a light blue pen, and then shook his head. It didn't matter. They all thought it.

He sat up and closed his eyes, pushing his fingertips into the bridge of his nose. When did everything get so darn dif-ficult? One minute he was rolling along and then *bam!* Evan showed up with his weird ideas and his Chinese soldiers. There weren't supposed to be Chinese soldiers in the Civil War.

It felt like somebody had to be lying. First, he thought Evan

187

was lying, but then Evan had shown that he wasn't, so now Brady had to consider the other possibility, which was that what he'd believed was a lie.

Well, Brady knew something about lying, didn't he? He laughed bitterly as he refolded the note.

"What's so funny?" Charlie was in the doorway, wiping the sleep out of his eyes. Charlie had been sleeping all day since he'd lost yet another job. This time he'd been employed all of three days before getting fired for talking back to a customer.

"Nothing," said Brady. It was better to respond quickly to Charlie, before his temper got up. That's what had gotten him fired. When Charlie had come home early from his shift, his dad shook his head and swore. "You're going to run out of places to work," Dad said.

"I'll open my own business," Charlie answered.

"You've got to have something to offer," said his dad. "You've got nothing. Actually worse than nothing. You've got a reputation."

"It's better than picking up dog crap all day," sneered Charlie.

That had sparked a whole round of screaming and threats, door-slamming and fingers jabbed in faces. Even though he had nothing to do with it, his father dragged Brady into it. "Don't turn out like this guy," he warned, pointing at Charlie. "He's a nothing. He's an embarrassment."

Brady screamed back, telling them both to shut up, but the real fight was between Dad and Charlie. He tried to fall asleep with Nero next to him, but every thump, every scream added to the pit in his stomach until he felt like he was carrying a pile of rocks in his gut. That's why he had stayed home from school the next day. Usually nothing kept Brady from school; it felt safer than home.

Nero whined and pushed against Brady's hands. Charlie took a step into the bedroom. "You ignoring me, boy?" he asked. Brady had not spoken loudly enough.

Brady slid the note into the tangle of sheets on his bed. "No, nothing's funny," he mumbled. Nero got to his feet and stood between Brady and Charlie. He thought quickly. "Unless prepositions are funny."

"Norwood still teaching that old stuff?" said Charlie. "About, above, across, after, against, ahead of, along . . ."

"You still remember?"

"Ingrained in my brain," said Charlie, tapping his temple.

"What else do you remember?" If Brady could get Charlie talking, maybe he'd work himself out of his bad mood.

"Oh, let's see. Some movie on foot hygiene. Reading some book about a raccoon. And Battlefield Day, of course."

"Who were you for Battlefield Day?"

"Jubal Griggs, of course. Are we ever anything else? Just like Dad and Uncle Peter. Good ol' Jubal Griggs, the one-legged legend." Charlie thumped his hands against the doorway, beating out a rhythm, and then disappeared.

It was a good question—are we ever anything else? And even their hero was kind of a bum. Brady leaned back on the bed and called Nero, letting the dog rest against his chest, letting Nero's weight settle him. He dug into the covers until he found the note again.

He took Nero for a walk first, to build up his courage. Brady liked walking, liked the way it made him feel. He often took Nero with him, but sometimes he just walked alone. Once he'd walked around the entire border of the town, from Martin's car dealership to the old Haddington house, once grand and now falling down, to Miller's field to Dalloway's ravine. This was a way of knowing a town, step by step.

Brady let his thoughts churn. He didn't owe anybody anything. He hadn't taken Evan's dog. But at the same time, he couldn't bear the thought of a lost dog, either. What would life be like without dogs? They didn't yell at you or get mad at you when you made mistakes. They just wanted some food, affection, and a walk now and then. Nero was the only one in the house who listened without criticizing him, who seemed excited when he came home.

If he could, if he thought anyone would understand, Brady would let everyone know why he was doing it, and it wasn't for their approval or their acceptance. But people saw what they wanted to see, that much had been made clear to him. No matter what he did, he was, and would be, the bad guy.

Don't turn out like this guy. His father's words came back to him, his dad stabbing his finger toward Charlie. Everyone thought he was turning out like Charlie, anyway. Maybe it wasn't worth trying not to.

Nero stopped, staring at his reflection in a puddle. Then he reared back on his hind legs and plunged his two front paws into the water, breaking the surface. Brady laughed. Nero was almost five, but still acted like a puppy sometimes. Nero jumped out of the puddle, dripping water everywhere.

"You're a mess," said Brady. "And that was your own reflection, not another dog."

He started to run with Nero, not for any particular reason, just to run and feel the wind against his face. To feel something else. The stretch of muscle, lungs burning. He turned back and watched the trail of paw prints turn from sloppy blotches to defined four-toed prints to only a faint outline. He'd walked around the edge of town, but could he ever run out?

Just do it, he told himself. Get it over with. It can't get any worse, right?

CHAPTER SEVENTEEN

EVAN

Evan didn't expect a knock at the back door, and he definitely didn't expect to find Brady Griggs there, doubled over, panting. A large black dog was with him.

Brady held a hand up. "I . . . didn't . . . take . . . your . . . dog . . ." he said between breaths.

Evan wasn't sure what to say. Under the rules of the silent treatment, he wasn't supposed to say anything. He held his hands up, palms facing the sky. Why was Brady telling him this?

Brady understood the gesture. He took one long breath and stood up. "Other people have been saying it. It's not true."

Evan nodded, not because he had some great belief in Brady, but because he knew what had actually happened: Mochi had opened the door in a panic. Also, he did not get the sense that

Brady was lying. "I know." It was a break in the silent treatment, but maybe just two words would not count.

What Brady said next, though, surprised him. "I can help you find her," Brady said.

He said it so confidently, the possibility of finding Mochi almost knocked the wind out of Evan. With every hour she was gone, the more it seemed like it would stay that way. He had gone to Miller's field after school, based on Julia's suggestion, and struck out. All he had gotten was the sense that Mochi could be anywhere.

But he didn't want Brady's help. It was too high a price to pay. He started to close the door. It was probably a trick, anyway.

"Wait," said Brady. "Are you just going to let your dog go then? You'd rather do that than get help from me?"

There was no gesture, no expression that Evan could conjure now. Fine. This was an emergency. Brady Griggs on his backdoor step was an emergency. "Why now? After everything you've done, why would you help now?" he asked.

Brady looked down at his dog. "I like dogs. And working with dogs is something I'm good at. I know how they think."

"You like dogs better than you like people," said Evan curtly.

"Dogs are less terrible than people," said Brady. The black dog sniffed at Evan. Evan's first instinct was to pull his hand away, but then he stopped. He wasn't angry with the dog. He held out his hand, letting the dog smell.

"Funny you should say that," said Evan. "A *dog* never shot at my house."

"The kids at school are saying I took your dog, and if it doesn't come back, they'll make the silent treatment permanent."

Evan snorted. "The truth comes out. You're offering to help because of the silent treatment."

"You just said you know I didn't take your dog," said Brady. "So you should know that's not why I'm doing this." He rubbed the back of his neck. "Look, do you want me to help? My dad says when a dog goes missing, you can't waste time. The longer you wait . . ."

Brady didn't finish the sentence but he didn't have to. Evan had already imagined all the terrible things that could have happened, things that kept Mochi from coming home. Still, he tried to keep his face neutral, his voice hard. "This better not be a trick." He didn't sense anything, no treachery. But Evan wondered if he could trust himself. He could already feel a tiny wisp of hope rise in his chest. Maybe they would find Mochi. But he squashed it back down. Hope had fooled him before.

"I'm not going to mess with you. Not when it comes to dogs." Brady stroked his dog's head. "That wouldn't be fair to Nero, either. What's your dog's name?"

Evan hesitated. "Mochi." Just saying her name made his heart ache a little.

"Mochi?"

"It's a dessert," Evan said defensively. Not exactly a tough-guy name, compared to Nero.

"Mochi," repeated Brady, smiling slightly.

"We're only talking so I can get my dog back," said Evan.

Brady said they needed something with Mochi's scent. Evan grabbed the towel they used to dry off Mochi when it rained. He told Celeste he was going for a walk. He didn't mention Brady. Celeste wouldn't have let him go.

Brady let Nero take a good sniff of the towel, turning it over and over and saying, "You want to go tracking, boy? Do you?" He spoke in a voice he never used at school, one that was warm and encouraging. When Nero had gotten excited,

Brady told him to track, and Nero started walking slowly up Carnegie, toward the school. To anybody watching, they might have looked like two friends taking a dog for a walk, thought Evan. Ha.

"That's it, good boy, Nero. Track!" Brady encouraged him.

Evan had decided not to tell Brady about Miller's field. He wanted to see where Nero would go, what the dog would do without being influenced. But they were headed in that direction, past the main entrance to the school to the other side of the school, over a small footbridge. Nero kept sniffing, sniffing, moving at a steady pace, occasionally stopping to smell a patch of grass or a telephone pole. Evan had never watched a dog follow a scent, the way they followed a path that was completely invisible to him, but clearly detecting something. What did they smell? Did they smell sneakers, too, and bicycle tires? How did Nero pick out one smell out of all the smells that landed on the ground?

Just as Evan was thinking that maybe Nero was on to something, though, he stopped at the old fire station. He lifted his head and inhaled, one, two, three times, walked around in a few circles, and looked at Brady.

"Why'd he stop?" Evan asked.

"Let's try the towel again," said Brady. He held out the towel again, trying to get Nero excited. Nero looked at the towel as if he'd never seen it. "He lost the scent, I guess."

Figures, thought Evan.

"Wait. There's a lot of concrete here. There's less for the scent to hold on to. Maybe she ran back across the water. Let's walk in a bigger circle."

They walked in larger and larger circles, letting Nero sniff. A man with a pink face, holding a can of soda, came out of his house and watched them. "You boys lose something?"

"Hi, Mr. Catten," said Brady. "Evan here lost his dog."

"You boys check Miller's field? Dogs seem to like it there; though you know the last time . . ."

"I think we're going there next," said Brady, cutting off the man suddenly. "That was my next idea." Mr. Catten did not seem to notice he had been interrupted. "Well, good luck to you," he said, heading back into the house. Brady thanked him, and the two boys turned to walk to the field.

"What was he going to say?" asked Evan. Brady had obviously not wanted Mr. Catten to say more.

"Don't worry about it," said Brady in a tone Evan was more accustomed to. Bossy, rough.

"I've been to Miller's field, and I didn't see anything," Evan warned him.

"What'd you do? Walk around, yelling for your dog?" asked Brady.

"I don't know what else you're supposed to do," said Evan. "So yeah."

Brady shook his head. "It's not enough to know where to look. You gotta know how to look. I just hope you didn't make too much of a mess."

Back where Evan lived in Schuyler, there were no spaces that were just fields. Every piece of land belonged to someone; every lot was supposed to be doing something. A dog park, a golf course, a baseball field. You had to have permission to use a space, and every field looked like it was managed because it was clean, no litter, recently mowed. But this field, this expanse of land, did not have that feeling. It was a wide field, filled with waist-high grass.

"How tall is Mochi?" asked Brady.

"This high?" Evan pointed to a spot halfway between his hip and his knee.

"So she could walk around in the grass and you wouldn't even see her," said Brady.

"But she'd come to me," said Evan. "She knows how to come."

"She knows to come to you if she's in her right mind. But sometimes dogs get nervous when they're out; they're not the same. Or maybe they ran because something scared them. And if she's like that, and you're stomping around, yelling her name, she's not going to come. She might run."

Evan started to point out that Mochi had not been the same since the shooting, and then stopped. Maybe that was the point of Brady's comment.

Brady pulled the towel out again and put it to Nero to smell. "C'mon, boy, let's have a sniff. Is Mochi here? Can you find Mochi?" This time Nero became more alert. He began to tug on the leash toward grass. Brady unclipped the leash and let Nero go ahead. All Evan could see was Nero's tail.

"Just be sure to check yourself for ticks when we leave here," said Brady. "They love it here." The boys walked slowly behind Nero, letting the dog take his time. The sky was darkening, threatening rain. What would Mochi do in the rain?

Nero stopped. Next to a large rock, the grass had been pushed down into a circle. "Something was taking a nap here," noted Brady. Nero sniffed the circle of grass intently.

"Keep going, boy," said Brady. "What else can we find?"

Nero pushed on, moving steadily toward the woods. The woods stretched out as far as Evan could see. *Please don't be in the woods*, he thought.

They came to a small clearing, an area where the grass did not grow. Brady pointed to a spot in a muddy patch. "I think there's a paw print," he said. "That looks like a dog's paw print, right?"

"I don't know what Mochi's paw print looks like," said Evan. To him, the ground just looked like peaks and valleys of mud, but if he looked hard enough, he could see something like a paw print. "I think it's about the right size, more or less."

"I think it's definitely a dog print," said Brady. "I like that." He squatted down and looked around. "Look, over there. See the way the grass bends like that? Looks like something's been making a tunnel, going back and forth. Maybe that's what Mochi's been doing."

"Or another dog," said Evan. "That man, Mr. Catten? He said dogs like coming here."

Brady nodded. "He did."

"Then he started to say something else."

"You don't want to know," said Brady.

Evan wasn't going to let Brady think he was the kind of person who was afraid to know things. "Yes, I do," he insisted.

Brady stood up, brushing off his hands. "You want to know? Fine. A little beagle got out here a few months ago and was killed by a coyote." Now Brady was mad. "They found the body over there, by the tree line. Just enough left to recognize him."

"Oh. That's awful."

"I know," said Brady. "Didn't have a chance."

Now Evan understood. Brady didn't want to think about Mochi in the same way. What would be worse—never knowing what happened to Mochi, or finding out something terrible had happened?

Brady put a hand up. "Don't move."

CHAPTER EIGHTEEN

BRADY

They were being watched.

Nero had stopped and lifted his front paw in the air, pointing toward the western end of the field. Brady scanned the grass, looking for the shape, the color that was out of place. Nothing on the first scan. He lowered his line of sight.

A dark eye, deep in the grass, stared back at him.

Brady told Evan about the eye. "Look for it, but don't stare. Staring is dominant behavior."

Evan glanced in the direction Brady told him to look. "I don't see anything."

"To be honest," said Brady. "I'm not one hundred percent sure it is Mochi, but it is something."

"So it could be anything," said Evan. "Like the coyote."

"Coyotes are usually light-eyed. I saw a dark eye. But either way, you've got to find out."

It started to rain. A light spring rain, patting down their hair, dampening their clothes. "If it isn't Mochi, we can keep tracking. Rain is good for that," he told Evan. "I wish we had some food."

"I have food," said Evan.

"You do?"

Evan reached into his pockets and pulled out a jerky stick and a granola bar. Brady smiled, almost involuntarily.

"What?" asked Evan.

"You always have food in your pockets?"

Evan shrugged, embarrassed. "I get hungry. Anyway, it's a good thing I brought some food, right?"

"I suppose. You're going to put on a big act on eating them, but at the same time, act like you don't care about whoever is there. Don't even look in that direction. I'd go with the granola bar first. Be sure to wrinkle the wrapper a lot. You're trying to get whatever it is to come closer."

"Unless I decide that it's something that I don't want to get closer," said Evan.

"Yeah, yeah. I'm going to take Nero and sit behind that

tree over there, and I'll tell you what to do. Set your phone on selfie mode, so you can pretend not to look at it, while still keeping an eye on it."

Brady told Evan to break open the granola bar and make lots of noise. "Make sure to drop some pieces on the ground," said Brady. "Be a messy eater. Make lots of noise so it knows that you're not trying to sneak up on it."

Evan sat down on the ground and tore open the granola bar. "Yummy granola," said Evan. "Yum yum yummy." He took a bite and then let bits of granola spill out of his mouth. Brady tried not to laugh.

"You said to be messy," said Evan.

"Didn't think you had it in you," said Brady, watching from behind the tree. "Slow down," said Brady. "You're going to get through that whole thing in a minute. You don't actually have to eat it, just pretend."

Evan began to exaggerate the eating motion. He dangled a chunk of granola over his mouth and then made loud chewing noises. "Good granola. Nom nom nom," he said. He peeked at his phone. "I still don't see anything."

"You have to wait," said Brady.

"How long?"

"As long as it takes," said Brady.

The rain picked up. Brady was protected by the tree, but Evan was getting completely soaked. He didn't complain, though. Brady thought of something.

"Could be a wolf. I think they can have darker eyes."

"I thought wolves were diurnal," said Evan.

Evan probably thought Brady didn't know what *diurnal* meant. Well, Brady could do him one better. "They're crepuscular," said Brady. When Evan looked confused, Brady added, "They're active at dusk and dawn." It was actually one of his favorite words, sounding weird and beautiful all at the same time.

"That's not exactly comforting, then," said Evan, dangling another chunk of granola near his mouth.

Nero whined. He wanted some food, too.

"Sorry, boy. I should have brought you something," said Brady.

"Here," said Evan. He tried to throw a piece of granola to Nero but fell short. At that moment, Brady spotted a movement in the grass.

"That might have gotten it moving," said Brady. "Lie down."

"What? Why?" said Evan.

"You have to be as unthreatening as possible," said Brady. "What's less threatening than a body on the ground?"

"I can think of things that are a lot more pleasant than being a body on the ground," said Evan. "In the rain." Evan lay partway down and continued to pantomime eating food. For a few minutes, neither one of them said anything. The wind picked up, sending waves across the grass. "This is taking a long time," said Evan.

"This isn't some store where you walk in and get what you want right away," said Brady. "You have to be patient."

"I thought I was being patient," said Evan. "But I'll stay here all day if I have to." He held up his phone to check, shielding it with one hand against the rain. "Wait—I think I see something."

Brady looked. A dark nose poked out of the grass, lifting and lowering, lifting and lowering. Brady moved back behind the tree.

"Calm voice," cautioned Brady. "Keep up the noisy eating."

"Here I am, lying in the grass, probably getting covered in ticks," said Evan. "I hope that's you, Mochi. Mmmm, should I move on to the jerky?" He took the meat out of the plastic casing. "Yummy yummy jerky."

"That wrapper doesn't make any noise, so you have to keep talking."

"This is turkey jerky. It is teriyaki-flavored. What else can I say? Was the person who invented jerky a jerk? Is that where it comes from? What if that person had been a nice person? Would we call it something else?" Evan babbled on.

The nose was moving. A dog emerged from the grass, about ten feet away from Evan. Plenty of room to jump away and run.

Evan drew a sharp breath. "It's her. It's Mochi," said Evan.

"Don't look," said Brady. He himself was so excited he wanted to shout. "You have to just let her be around you. Keep dropping food."

"Why can't I just grab her?"

"Cause she's way faster than you are," said Brady. "And then she won't trust you."

Evan put one hand over his eyes. "I'm not going to look," Evan announced. "If I look, I'll get too excited," he said.

Brady stayed in view by the side of the tree, keeping watch, occasionally offering reports. "She's almost at your feet." "Hey! She ate a piece of the jerky." Poor Nero, he had to watch all of this without getting any food. "I'm going to give you the best dinner when we get home," Brady told him.

For ten long minutes, Mochi inched closer, vacuuming up bits of food around Evan. Then Brady saw the sign he'd been hoping for. Her mouth opened slightly, like a smile.

"You can look," said Brady. "But not stare." Evan opened one eye, slightly and smiled. "Hey, girl." He looked away, to Brady, and nodded.

"See if she'll come touch you," said Brady. "Put a piece of jerky really close to you."

Evan put a piece of jerky in the palm of his hand, and let it open loosely on the ground. Mochi sniffed and then jumped away slightly. When Evan didn't move, she came back and took the jerky with the tips of her front teeth. After she ate it, she came back and nudged Evan's hand as if asking for more.

Evan lifted his hand and let it drop slowly against Mochi, as if petting her by accident. He did it again. And again.

"It's me, Mochi," he murmured. "Do you remember me now?"

Now he was petting her with more deliberate strokes, parceling out tiny bits of jerky. "Don't rush now," said Brady. If she ran off, they'd have to start over again.

"I'm not," said Evan. Brady could hear him talking low under his breath. Mochi seemed to lean in, as if listening, and

209

then licked his hand. She seemed to recognize him now. Her tail wagged slightly. Evan reached out, and lightly grasped Mochi's collar.

"Got her," he said, his voice quietly triumphant. He slowly got to his feet and looked at his phone. "That took over an hour." He leaned over and talked to Mochi. "It took an hour but felt like a million years."

"Oh come on," said Brady. "Only a thousand." Brady looked down and realized his hand was shaking.

"Let's go home," Evan said to Mochi. "Let's go home."

CHAPTER NINETEEN

EVAN

The emergency is over, Evan reminded himself.

It was hard to remember in a moment of so much happiness that he should not talk to Brady. He wanted to carry Mochi all the way home. He wanted to smell her wet, stinky fur and feel the reassuring heft of her weight in his arms. He wanted to walk in the front door, triumphantly, with Mochi. At least, he did want these things until he realized how heavy and wiggly she was.

He wanted to share the moment. Rehash what happened. Revel in the highlights.

Brady grunted his approval when Evan put her down on the ground and attached the leash that Brady had loaned him. He probably thought that carrying Mochi was stupid, like carrying a stuffed animal. Evan tried to turn that into a reason to hate Brady, but he couldn't. He wasn't mad at Brady anymore. He felt defective. What was wrong with him? People fought whole wars. Couldn't he at least do a silent treatment?

Brady shot a gun at the house, he reminded himself. He hurt Mochi. He hurt all of them, just not all in a physical way.

Brady interrupted his thoughts. "Listen, don't tell anyone about this, okay?"

"By 'this,' you mean . . . ?"

"Finding the dog, of course," said Brady. "This is between you and me. And the dogs."

So Brady seemed ready to go back to not talking. Maybe he didn't feel the same way, though he had seemed plenty excited a few minutes ago. Still, it was probably for the best. How could he even explain this to Max? At least, maybe Brady would leave him alone, once the silent treatment was over. They could go to neutral.

Then again, if Brady had left him alone a few hours ago, he wouldn't have Mochi now.

"I think if people knew you helped me, that would be . . . fair," said Evan. He didn't say all the other pieces, about ending the silent treatment, ending the threat of permanent silent treatment, but Brady understood.

He stopped walking. "No, that's not why I did it. I told you that. Your dog is home. Just tell people she came home and leave me out of it." He made a motion with his hands, a flat line. Evan was confused.

"You're doing this to make up for the window," said Evan. And there it was, a little residual flare of anger. It felt safe, like a shield.

"Sure," said Brady. "If that's what you want to believe."

They had this moment between them. This moment where Evan had felt as alive as he ever had, lying in the grass, in the rain, trying to convince his dog to come back to him, and they were never going to talk again. If they were really going to stop, act as if this never happened, Evan wanted to ask one more question. The question that never got answered.

"Why'd you do it?" he asked. "Why'd you shoot my window?"

Brady fumbled. "You . . . you . . ."

"Don't start with 'you.' I didn't do anything," said Evan. "You know I didn't. I never did anything but be myself." His voice rose. Mochi looked back at him, worried. Evan hated himself. For wanting an answer only Brady could give. For needing an answer.

"I just did," said Brady. "You messed up everything. Everything was going to be great, and then you rolled in." He made his voice nasally, pretending to be Evan. "I'm so smart; I'm so great. I found stuff about the Civil War that even the teacher didn't know." He cleared his throat. "I was mad. I just did it."

Then there it was, like a punch between the eyes. For a moment, Evan couldn't see anything, then he shook his head, trying to get clear. It was a doozy. He hadn't felt one like this in a long time.

"You're lying," he said. His mind started to race. Here's where things got tricky. Evan could sense when people were lying, but he didn't always know what they were lying about.

"I am not!" said Brady. "Why would I lie?" Which only sent another punch right to Evan's brain.

"I never said I'm so great," said Evan, trying to find the lie.

"You don't have to," said Brady. "You act like it."

Evan stopped to steady himself against a tree next to the sidewalk. Amazingly, Brady stayed with him. Maybe Evan was too involved. Maybe his detector was off completely. Just

214

like with Dad. Mochi pulled him to the other side of the tree, going after a smell.

For a second, Brady disappeared behind the tree.

Brady. Tree. Brady. Tree.

Something was trying to click, like a switch that would not quite catch and hold. But he was getting close. Brady. Tree. Brady. Tree.

Brady in the field, shielded by the tree. Calling out directions from the tree.

Evan stepped around the tree so he was directly in front of Brady. "Where did you say you were when you fired the gun?"

Brady hesitated. "Bedroom," he said.

"Your bedroom?"

"No, your mom's bedroom," snapped Brady.

"Have you . . . have you always had the same room in your house?"

"Charlie's not exactly dying to have the smallest room in the house," said Brady. He turned abruptly and walked ahead, Nero following obediently behind him. Evan walked a few paces behind. They passed the school, headed down the long hill. They passed Max's street. The rain had stopped and the sweet smell of earth rose up. The streets glistened.

It was Max's story. *He climbed out his bedroom window, shimmied down the tree.* Brady. Tree. The road curved and Brady's house came into view. Evan looked, to be sure, but he already knew. There were no trees in the front of Brady's house. A tall gray tree peeked over the roofline from the back of the house. The back, not the front.

"You didn't do it," Evan said. It wasn't a question.

"Just stop. Shut up." Brady raised his chin, trying to keep his advantage up. But Evan could see all the cracks inside. The throbbing in his head stopped. The picture had snapped into place.

"You don't know everything," said Brady.

"I know what side of the house you need to be on to see my house, and it's not the side with the tree," Evan said.

Brady speed-walked ahead and then turned around. "You got what you wanted. You got your dog back. Everyone at school hates me. You even have a Civil War . . . thing. What more do you want?" His words came out like stomps. What. More. Do. You. Want. "I just wanted to do this one thing, this one thing and keep it pure, and you have to go and mess that up, too."

"Why would you take the blame . . ." Brady didn't let Evan finish.

The NO MERCY car turned onto Carnegie from the opposite side, from the main road. Brady broke into a run toward his house, Nero racing beside him. "Don't come near me," he half shouted. "We're done talking."

Evan couldn't tell if it was a threat or a plea.

Mochi's feet didn't touch the ground for the first hour she was home. Mom and Celeste just kept holding her and kissing her. For her part, Mochi was pretty willing to soak it all in. Celeste took approximately three thousand pictures of her. When Mom asked how Evan found her, he just said, "Someone told me to check Miller's field."

"Did they tell you to get soaking wet, too?" Mom made him take a hot shower before dinner and put on socks and slippers afterward. "Be sure to keep your feet warm," she told him. "If your feet are warm, the rest of you will be warm."

Mom cooked some chicken and then divided it between plates for the people and Mochi. Mom put Mochi's bowl right next to her chair and added some rice. It felt comfortable. The room felt good and warm and complete.

"Anyone home?" said a voice. It was Uncle Joe. "Come in,

come in," said Mom. "We were just sitting down to dinner." She got out a pair of slippers for him and told Evan to set another place.

Evan tried to soak it in. The goodness, the feeling of home. Uncle Joe was there now. Just think of the good things, he told himself. Mochi was home. But Brady nagged at him. He'd finally gotten the answer to his question, *why'd you do it*, and gotten more than he'd bargained for. A whole unspooling of different events than he'd expected.

There was one other person he wanted to ask that question— *why'd you do it?* Dad. They had picked up their lives and moved on, but the question had left a hole inside of him. Why had he taken the money? Why had he left them behind? He wished he could be as hard as the words he'd said in the car that day—*I don't care.* But he did. It was his curse.

They spent the evening finishing up the costume for Battlefield Day. A pair of jeans would have to do for the bottom, and Evan had black sneakers instead of boots, but that was okay, he convinced himself. The main part was the jacket. "Did you find gold buttons for the jacket?" asked Evan. Mom nodded. "Can you show me how to sew them on?"

"I can do it for you," said Mom. "It would be quicker. And

you won't have to worry about pricking your finger." She had already gotten out her sewing box and picked out a spool of dark blue thread.

"But I want to do it," said Evan. "I want to know how to do it." Mom raised her eyebrows. "Okay, then," she said. "I'll show you."

She showed him how to thread the needle and knot the ends together, and then how to stitch the button to the coat. Evan sewed a single row of buttons along the edge of the jacket flap, careful to keep the buttons in a neat row. He only stuck his finger a few times, pushing the needle through the thick cloth. But something was still missing.

"I have an idea of how to make one of those caps," said Celeste. "All we need is a baseball cap to sacrifice."

"You're going to help?" asked Evan. "I thought you said this was weird."

"It is weird," said Celeste. "But I'm not going to let you look like a fool. It's too important."

Celeste cut back the brim on a baseball cap, and then pushed down the crown of the hat with a circle of cardboard. She covered the whole thing with some dark blue felt and added a black strip across the front. "Amazing what you can do with a glue gun," she said.

219

Celeste wouldn't let him look in the mirror until she finished the cap. She made him walk backward into the bathroom and put the cap on him. She stood back and appraised him first. She closed one eye and cocked the cap to one side. "Not bad."

"Okay, now look," she commanded. She grasped him by the shoulders and turned him around.

For a brief second, Evan didn't recognize himself. An older person stared back at him. Serious eyes peeked out under the cap. His shoulders looked broader under the coat. "I look like them," he said. The few precious images he had seen. Joseph Pierce. Edward Day Cohota. Hong Neok Woo. Plus all the other people he could only imagine, their faces lost to time. The ones who had lost their lives, fighting for a country they believed in. A future they believed in.

That was their legacy. It wasn't just having them in the past, as a stake to say *we were here*, that mattered. It was their story, carrying Evan into the future. *We are here, and we're here to stay. We're here to fight for the country that is yet to be.*

Mom joined them in the bathroom, looking at Evan in the mirror. Thinking of the soldiers had made him brave.

"I want . . ." Evan slowed down, trying to choose his words

carefully. He did not want to hurt Mom, or anyone. But he had his own needs. "I think I want to talk to Dad, about what happened."

Mom reached over and cut off a piece of thread with her silver scissors. Snip. "You have to be careful. Dad has not been honest."

"I know that," said Evan. "I know that more than anyone."

"I just want to keep you guys safe," said Mom. "You've already been through a lot."

"I don't want the kind of safety that's fake, though. Not the kind of safety from not knowing the truth," said Evan. "I want to know the truth." He looked over at Celeste, half expecting her to yell at him. She didn't say anything, but her head nodded, the tiniest bit.

Mom let out a long breath. "Let's go slowly, okay?"

"As long as I can do something," said Evan. "Maybe write a letter?"

Mom nodded. "That might be a start."

It was one start. There was still another truth he had to contend with.

* * *

221

Getting to the first branch of the tree was the hardest part. It was about seven feet off the ground. If he could get to that branch, everything else would be easy.

Nero had sniffed at him and wagged his tail when Evan snuck into the backyard. Evan had come prepared for that. He gave the dog a piece of chicken from dinner, and petted him. He had the leash with him, figuring that if he got busted, he could say that he was returning Nero's leash. He had to get up the tree.

He tried bear-hugging the trunk to get to the first branch. Jumping. Running up the side at full speed. Nothing. Evan sat on the ground panting. Maybe it was a sign that it wasn't meant to happen. Nero pawed at him. He probably thought he was entitled to a walk because of the leash.

A walk. The leash. Evan held the leash in front of him, and then threw the leash over the branch. It was just long enough. He grabbed the end with the handle and attached the clip. Now he had a loop around the branch. Slowly, slowly, wishing he had more muscle, Evan pulled himself up to the first branch. Now the trick was not to look down. He reached up and grasped the next branch. Evan focused on moving upward, feeling the distance growing between himself and the

222

earth. The tree started to sway as he went up. This was crazy. But he couldn't shake the feeling again. Not even Mochi could help him this time. This was the only way.

Brady's bedroom was small, barely large enough for a bed and a chair, covered with dirty clothes. Brady was sitting on his bed, playing a video game.

"Brady," said Evan. Brady did not hear him.

Evan scooted along the branch that went closest to Brady's window. The branch began to dip so low Evan thought it might snap off. He clung to the branch and quickly tapped on the window.

Brady looked up and dropped the game. Quickly, he shut the door to his room and then slid the window open.

"Are you nuts?" Brady whisper-shouted. "What are you doing here?"

"We need to talk," said Evan.

"I don't have to talk to you," said Brady. He was still shout-whispering and glancing over his shoulder toward the door. "And you're not supposed to talk to me, remember?"

"This is an emergency," said Evan.

"You on that branch is an emergency," said Brady. "Go back toward the tree trunk."

223

Evan scooted back and the branch rose up. "Don't you ever just get tired of not talking about the truth?" asked Evan.

Brady sighed and closed the door to his room slightly. Then he lifted the screen, leaned out the opening, and grabbed a higher branch, slightly above the window. He hoisted himself out of the window, and then made his way to Evan.

Evan wrapped his arm around the tree trunk as the tree swayed from Brady's movement. "You do this a lot?" asked Evan, trying to hide the fear in his voice.

"Enough," said Brady. "But this is the first time someone has climbed up here to me." He paused, thinking. "How'd you make it to the first branch?"

"I used the leash," said Evan. "Threw it over the branch and made a loop to grab on to."

Brady nodded, as if approving. "There used to be a lower branch, good for climbing." Then an awkward silence began to fill the space between them. It was now or never, thought Evan.

"I want to know the whole story," Evan said. "Everything."

"Huh," said Brady. "You want the whole story? Of my life? Try being a Griggs in this town. We peaked in the 1800s and it's been downhill ever since."

"I'm not sure Jubal Griggs was a peak," said Evan. Then

224

he covered his mouth. He'd forgotten the desertion paper was a secret.

"Huh, it was you who put that paper in my lunch," said Brady. "I should have figured." He laughed, bitterly. "He did come back, just so you know. He didn't walk away and stay away. He just needed to take care of his family for a while."

"What about you, though?" Evan tried again. "If you didn't do it, you shouldn't take the blame."

Brady let out a long breath. "It might as well have been me," said Brady. "It was as good as me." He said this as if that made everything else make sense.

Evan's skin prickled. "So you admit it wasn't you."

Brady sighed. He pointed to one of the windows on the lower floor. "My brother Charlie's down there. You see him?"

Evan leaned back on the branch to get a look. "I can see someone moving." Shadows and light shifted. Someone was watching TV in the dark.

Brady grabbed the branch overhead and rested his head on his forearms. "Charlie will be nineteen next month." When Evan didn't say anything, Brady added. "Charlie is an adult."

Evan wasn't sure how to respond. "My sister, Celeste, is going to be sixteen."

225

"No," interrupted Brady. "You don't get it. If an adult shoots at a house, he's going to court and probably jail, especially if he's already known as a troublemaker like Charlie Griggs. Even if his dad knows some of the guys on the force. But a kid? Like me? It's definitely a better deal."

Evan puzzled out what Brady was saying. "You're saying that Charlie shot at our house."

Brady nodded, barely. He stared into the darkness. "You went to the council meeting and talked about those Chinese soldiers. It made him so mad. And then he lost his job, again." Brady rubbed his face against his arm. "I was home sick that day, remember? I was walking by his room and he said, 'Hey, Brady, come watch this.' He already had the window open." Brady paused. "Charlie already had his rifle out. I said, 'What are you doing?' He said, 'I'm just reminding some folks who's in charge.' I said, 'Don't do it.' He said, 'Nobody's home. Whose side are you on?'"

Evan felt like he was watching a movie. With each description, he was there, with Brady.

Brady shook the branch he was holding. "He kept pretending to fire the gun, to mess with me. He'd look through the scope like he was going to fire for real, and then he'd turn and

226

shout, 'BANG!' Right in my face. He thought it was so funny. And then I thought, maybe he won't do it. Then he did, he pulled the trigger, and then he stopped laughing. He looked at me, and he said, 'I'm doing this for you.'"

Brady stared into the darkness. "At that point, all I could think was, nobody's home. That was like the only thing that kept me from losing it. I just kept thinking, nobody was home. That's what I was thinking when the police showed up."

"And then you went along with taking the rap," said Evan.

Brady nodded. "Yeah. Dad didn't give me much choice. He said they wouldn't give me too bad a time, but Charlie? They've cut him some slack, but this probably wasn't something they could let slide." Brady brushed his hair out of his eyes. "At first, I was mad, but then I thought, that's gonna be me, anyway. That's where all this is going. With enough time, it's going to be me taking that shot. So what's the difference between me and Charlie? I'm just takin' my punishment a few years early." Brady let out a hard laugh. "Some punishment. Even Dad was surprised we didn't go down to the station."

"You were surprised," said Evan, emphasizing the *you*. "It was like they didn't even think about us."

227

Nero looked up the tree at them and barked. A light came on and a door opened. Nero went inside.

"But when I found out that Mochi was in the house, that she could have been shot, or even just scared, that stopped me. I didn't want any part of that." Brady took in a deep breath. "I had to do something right. Something good."

"You did," said Evan. As soon as he said the words, Evan scolded himself. *Stop being nice.* Even if Brady had not pulled the trigger, there was a reason why it had seemed possible. "Though you've still done plenty of terrible things. To me." Flag football. The swing at Dalloway ravine. *Do you have the China virus?*

Brady stood up on the branch, grabbed for the one he had used to get out of the window and shook it. "It's not right. It's not right," he said. Evan wasn't sure what the *it* was. Was it what Brady had done, or what Evan had done? Brady let go of the upper limb, letting it snap back to place, and stood up on the branch. He held his arms out, a perfect T balanced on top of a slender branch.

Evan froze, not daring to move. *Please don't fall.* Then he had a worse thought. *Please don't jump.* "What are you doing?" asked Evan, barely daring to move his mouth.

228

"I'm seeing if I'm ready to fly," said Brady. His voice was almost playful.

"Please," said Evan. "Don't." His arms tensed. If Brady started to jump, maybe he'd get one shot at grabbing him. A few days ago, if you'd told him that Brady could disappear from view, he might have said *good*. But now Evan's entire being was focused on making sure Brady sat back down.

Evan thought of something. "Wait. You want a cookie? A Fig Newton? These packages come with two." Evan pushed his hip out, rebalancing himself on the branch, reached into his pocket and pulled out a yellow package.

"A Fig Newton?" Brady said.

"Who doesn't like a Fig Newton?" *I hope you do*, he thought. If food had worked for Mochi, maybe it would work here. "They have all these different flavors, but I still like fig the best. It's a classic. Did you know that they're over one hundred years old? It's kind of squished, but it's all the same in your stomach." Keep talking. Keep talking.

Brady didn't say anything. He didn't even look at Evan. Then he bent his knees and then reached out and clasped a smaller limb, one that Evan had not seen in the dark. He sat down. Evan leaned against the trunk and exhaled. He tore

229

open the package with his teeth and held it out to Brady. Brady took one cookie.

Brady's mouth twisted. "My mama used to say that. It's all the same in your stomach." He took a bite.

"Doesn't everyone's mom say that? That and, if everyone jumped off a bridge, would you do it, too?" Evan was still jabbering, trying to make sure his words kept Brady tethered to the tree.

Brady tore off a piece of Fig Newton. "I don't know what else she says. She's not around anymore."

"Oh," Evan had not expected that. "My dad's not around, either," Evan heard himself say. Funny. Brady was just about the last person he thought he'd say that to.

Brady grunted, a sound of recognition. "Sucks, doesn't it?"

"It does," said Evan. "It does."

For a moment, neither boy said anything. The tree gave Evan a new perspective of the town, seeing the shapes of roofs of the houses below, seeing the lights of trucks going by.

"Why do you care so much, anyway? You should hate me. I've done plenty to warrant that," said Brady.

Evan didn't answer right away. "You have," said Evan. "But

that doesn't mean I don't care about the truth now." It was more than that, though. He knew it from that moment when Brady stood teetering on the branch. He wanted Brady to live.

Brady snorted. "The truth." He made air quotes.

"What?" said Evan. "The truth matters."

Brady shook his head. "No, it doesn't. If you tell the kids at school that I helped find Mochi, they'll say it's because I had taken her and I knew where she was all along. If I tell the truth about Charlie, well, I better say it while I'm running so I get a head start on him. Maybe my dad, too." Brady looked at Evan. "You cannot tell a soul about Charlie. I'm as serious as a heart attack."

"It can't be like that," said Evan. "The truth matters. I'll tell 'em the truth, that Mochi got out on her own and you helped me find her."

"Then they'll want to know why I helped if I had nothing to do with it, because Brady Griggs wouldn't do something just because it was right. And if you tell them why I helped, then we're back to telling on Charlie," said Brady. His face softened for a moment. "Even if I wanted to change, no one would let me."

"Brady," said Evan.

Brady wouldn't let him finish. In one quick movement, he moved toward the window and slid back into his room. He turned around, hesitating. "I am sorry. I'm sorry for all of it. I was wrong about you." Then he closed the window and turned out the light.

CHAPTER TWENTY

MAX

The morning of Battlefield Day started cool and clear. Max had spent the night on the sleeping porch and woke up to the sound of birds. He'd been looking forward to Battlefield Day as long as he could remember. When he was a kid, it just seemed fun—getting to put on the uniforms and stay outside all day, going to the different stations and talking to people. Today, though, felt like it meant more than that.

"Morning." Mama joined him on the porch in her bathrobe, carrying a cup of coffee. "You ready for today?"

Max sat up and stretched. "As ready as I'll ever be." He padded over to her and leaned up against her, still waking up. Being a middle child, Max rarely got to have a quiet moment with his mom. Usually he was in the thick of the scrum, competing with his brothers for attention.

"You have a good day for it. When it was your brother Clark's turn, it was so hot one of the kids passed out. Those uniforms are hot." She took a sip of her coffee. "Just stay hydrated. Tell your friends. I'm supposed to be running the sloosh station over the fire, have mercy."

"What's going to happen after this year? Are they still going to have Battlefield Day after Mrs. Norwood retires?" asked Max.

"That is the subject of much debate among the school moms. None of the other teachers want to do all that work, that's for sure. But tradition, right? Also, Jacob will pitch a fit if he doesn't get a turn."

"You could probably bribe him with a trip to Kings Dominion instead," said Max. Kings Dominion was the amusement park they went to every summer.

"Right? Oooh, that's tempting. Probably only a little more crying and throwing up than Battlefield Day." Max laughed. "But seriously, here's my question. We do all this work, with the fire and the tents and the food. And I know you guys love it, but do you actually learn something, or is it all fun and games?"

Max paused, thinking about his mom's comment. "I mean, I learned about the Chinese soldiers, although that was before Battlefield Day."

"Oh, you mean the thing with Evan? That's really nice for him, but what's something you learn that matters? That's like . . ." She fluttered her fingers in the air. "Not trivia, exactly, but you know what I mean."

"Mama, it matters. It's not just a thing for Evan." Max was a little shocked his mother would say that, but maybe she had to be there, to be in the class.

"Mmmm . . . maybe." Mama took another sip of coffee.

"My whole idea of what the war looked like, and who fought, it changed because of Evan. Other kids, too. Maybe you might think it's some story off to the side, because you hadn't heard it before," said Max.

Mom pursed her lips. "That's true, I suppose. Maybe Evan could talk to me about his profile and I can learn some more."

"Um, but don't embarrass me, okay? Like, just, don't."

"When have I embarrassed you?" Mom asked.

When he was younger, Max loved having his mom at school, but recently, it seemed like a dicier proposition. A few weeks ago she had come in to help with the book fair, and she had waved with her whole arm in front of everyone. Her whole arm for everyone to see!

"You want your answer in alphabetical or chronological order?" deadpanned Max.

"Oh, git." She smacked him lightly on the bottom. "You better go get ready for school. I'll see you at the sloosh."

Max raised a fist in the air. "Slooosh!"

"What is sloosh?" asked Evan.

Evan, Casey, Julia, and Max had worked their way around the different stations at Battlefield Day, getting their pictures taken and looking at the medical kits. They had taken turns crawling inside a white canvas tent that made Max feel slightly claustrophobic. It was a great day so far, especially when Evan said his dog had come home. Now they could just have fun. Mrs. Norwood had assigned them to groups so they would rotate and not clump up at one station or another. Sloosh was next on the list but it had already become a word of the day. When they had been at the coding station, all of their messages were about sloosh, mostly to get on Max's case, and because *sloosh* was fun to say.

"Send . . . more . . . sloosh . . ." said Evan, decoding Julia's message.

"Save . . . our . . . sloosh . . ." said Casey, writing out another one.

The sloosh station radiated heat from the fire. Mama was sweating, keeping the fire running, waving off the smoke. She showed them how to make sloosh. She cooked bacon in a pan, then added cornmeal to the grease. Once it became doughlike, she wrapped it around a straight stick, which was supposed to be like the ramrod the soldiers used, and cooked it over the fire.

"Can we have a piece of bacon?" asked Evan. He was practically drooling over the cake pan that Mama was filling up with slices of cooked bacon. Mama shook her head. "Sorry, boys, just the grease for sloosh. Also, if I give you bacon, I have to have enough for everyone else."

Evan stared at the pile of bacon sadly. "Don't let it go to waste, okay?"

Mama winked. "Some of this might end up at my house. You're just going to have to come over again."

Sloosh turned out to be one of the more delicious parts of the meal. Evan recognized Mrs. Hoover, the real estate agent, as she passed out pieces of hardtack, which were about as tasty

237

as cardboard. She spotted Evan. "Look at you," she said. "You look great! Fitting right in!"

"Thank you," said Evan. If his cheeks were not already red from the heat, they would be red from blushing.

"Why'd they make these crackers so hard," asked Casey, gnawing on a square. "If I break my braces, my mom's going to kill me."

"Soldiers soaked them in stew," said Mrs. Hoover. "Let 'em soften. But you kids never want the stew so we just stuck with hardtack."

"If this is what they gave soldiers, what did they give prisoners?" asked Casey. Mrs. Hoover didn't know. They moved on to the next station under a large tree, where Mr. Catten was in charge of dried apples. The shade from the tree was a relief. "More soldiers died of disease than battle injuries in the Civil War," Mr. Catten told them. "Scurvy made it hard for the men to march and fight because it made their joints hurt. Apples prevent scurvy because they have vitamin C." He handed each of them a small wax paper bag with apples in them. "Hey, did you and your friend find your dog?" He was talking to Evan.

Evan seemed to freeze. "Yes, we did. Thanks," he said. He

stood up and moved away from the shade of the tree. The group followed him.

"Someone helped you find Mochi?" asked Max. He had thought Evan was alone when he found Mochi.

Evan looked straight at Max. "Yeah. Brady Griggs."

Max laughed. "Yeah, right. And Abraham Lincoln helped me with my profile." Max looked across the playground and spotted Brady. He had drifted away from his group. He was eating by himself along the fence.

"It's the last day," said Evan.

"You mean, for the silent treatment," said Max. Evan nodded. It seemed like the silent treatment had done its job, putting Brady in check. "Yeah. Everything goes back to normal on Monday."

"I'd rather not," said Evan. "Have everything go back to normal. The way it was."

"I mean, not like that," said Max. "I hope he learned his lesson and Brady will leave you alone."

"What if I don't?" asked Evan.

"You don't want Brady to leave you alone?" said Max, raising his eyebrows.

"What if I want something different?" asked Evan.

CHAPTER TWENTY-ONE

EVAN

Evan started walking across the blacktop, straight for Brady.

Brady looked at him and shook his head slightly. When Evan didn't stop, Brady made a small brushing motion with his hand. *Don't come here.* Finally, Evan stopped, letting his shadow fall over Brady. Brady looked away. "You're going to get us both in trouble."

"Calm down," said Evan.

"If you leave right now, you can say you just went crazy from the heat. Go. Just go." Brady wouldn't even look at him. He was talking without moving his mouth, like a ventriloquist.

"The silent treatment was because of me," said Evan. "I think I should get to have some say in when it ends. Or how it ends." He sat down next to Brady, letting his back press into the chain-link fence. Evan felt relaxed, calm, even though Brady was freaking out. Max had followed him halfway across the playground before stopping.

"Don't be scared," said Evan. Brady's emotions threatened to overwhelm his own. Evan took a deep breath. He was going to handle this. His way. The way where he felt the bravest, the most sure.

Other kids noticed Brady and Evan together. First, they just stared, then they began to edge closer.

"What going on?" asked Julia. The kids turned to look at Max, who nodded toward Brady and Evan.

"Children!" said Mrs. Norwood. She swished onto the blacktop in a dark gray dress that went all the way to the ground. "You're supposed to be on the schedule, not gathering here."

"Wait," said Evan. He had to think fast, so the group wouldn't break up. "I have a question about the Civil War. The end part." He looked at the faces of those around him, taking in their feelings. Curious, surprised, interested. Some seemed a little annoyed.

"Oh?" Mrs. Norwood looked around the blacktop. Now the adults were watching with interest. "Well, I suppose that would be appropriate on Battlefield Day." The volunteers chuckled lightly.

"When the war ended, how did people get to where they could be neighbors again?"

"Not sure they have," said one of the parents.

"Lee surrendered to Grant at Appomattox, and the other armies of the Confederacy followed," said Mrs. Norwood, almost automatically.

"I don't mean surrender," said Evan. "That just means you agree not to kill each other. I mean something else." Evan couldn't quite put his feelings into words. "I mean, like actually figure out how to get along in the future. Maybe someone apologized."

"That's not usually how wars end," said Mrs. Norwood. Some of the adults covered up smiles. "Governments don't normally apologize."

Evan saw his opening. "People do, though," said Evan. "And people figure stuff out together. People apologize. And people forgive." He stood up and turned back to Brady, offering him a hand up. Brady hesitated, then clasped Evan's hand to stand. For a brief second, Brady was completely at Evan's mercy, his balance dependent on Evan's grip before he stood up. Then he leaned slightly forward and let go. A murmur of surprise rippled across the playground.

Mrs. Norwood was unaware of what had just transpired. She clapped her hands. "Let's return to the stations now, shall we? Get back in your groups, please."

"You're in for it now," said Brady under his breath. "You chose the wrong side." Max, Casey, and Sophia joined them. Evan thought Max might be mad.

"Why do I feel like the silent treatment has been broken already?" Max asked. He didn't sound mad—just confused.

"It was an emergency," said Evan.

"It must have been," said Sophia. "For this to happen." She gestured from Evan to Brady, then back to Evan. Brady jammed his hands in his pockets and looked at the ground.

"What happened?" asked Max. Brady looked at Evan urgently and shook his head slightly. Max's eyes widened. "When I asked you . . ."

"What you need to know," said Evan, interrupting Max, "is that Brady has apologized and I've forgiven him. Everything else is just details." He gestured between Brady and himself. "We've worked it out." Brady nodded, hunching his shoulders.

"I was wrong about a lot of things," said Brady. "About Evan."

243

It felt like the whole group exhaled at the same time. Forgiveness was enough. Forgiveness was its own kind of truth.

"Okay," said Max. "Okay. We're done."

"I wouldn't say done," said Evan. "I'd say beginning. There's at least one more thing Brady needs to do."

Brady lifted his head. "What's that?"

CHAPTER TWENTY-TWO

BRADY

"You know your mother is terrifying, right?" asked Brady as they stood on the front porch.

"You climb in and out of a tree that's taller than your house, take the rap for your brother in front of the police, and you're scared of *my* mom?" asked Evan.

"Yes," said Brady.

"Have you met your dad?" asked Evan.

"I know what my dad's going to do," said Brady.

"She's not going to do anything to you physically," said Evan. "Though you might feel a little scorched when she's done talking to you."

"Tell me again, why am I doing this?" Brady could see his

house from Evan's porch. It would take nothing at all to jump down and run home. But he stayed.

"One, you need to make things right with my mom, so then two, you can come over," said Evan. Before Brady could change his mind, Evan opened the door to the house. "Mom?"

"In here." The voice was very close. Too close. Brady forced himself to step into the house. Evan's mom was sitting on the couch with her legs tucked up, petting Mochi. When she saw Brady, though, she stood up quickly. Mochi ran over and jumped happily on Brady.

"Brady is here to talk to you," said Evan. Evan said he would tell his mom that Brady was coming, but she still seemed upset.

"Hello, Ms. Pao," said Brady, petting Mochi. She nodded, not saying anything. She seemed surprised by Mochi's reaction.

Evan nudged Brady. This was the hard part. Brady knew plenty about war; he knew a lot less about apologies.

He let the words come out in a flurry, the words they had practiced. "I am coming over to apologize for the harm I have caused your family," he said. "I hope you will forgive me." Brady and Evan had worked out the words so they were still truthful. He had caused harm; he knew that now. He was sorry.

Almost reflexively, they both turned their heads to look at the window. In his mind, Brady could still picture the cracks, the gap in the glass. Evan's mom narrowed her eyes. "You could have killed someone," she said coldly. "Someone in my family." She shook her head. "I can't believe you weren't arrested."

That makes two of us, Brady wanted to say. "No one was hurt," said Brady. "But my intentions were not good." What had someone said to him the first day he met Evan, the day he had asked if Evan had the China virus? Words like that have killed people. It seemed truer now than it did then. "And now I want to do better. By you."

"You can't do those things," said Ms. Pao. She looked down. Her hand was curled into a fist. She unclenched her hand and took a step so that she was standing right in front of Brady. She was smaller than Brady, but he was the one who felt vulnerable. "When does it stop?"

Brady swallowed. "With me, it stops now. I hope you can find it in your heart to forgive me." He closed his eyes. This is usually the point where Dad started calling him names.

You're stupid. No-good. Irresponsible. The waiting was as bad as anything.

"And you won't do those things," she said, stressing the future tense. "Not ever again."

"No, ma'am," said Brady. "I will not." He also emphasized the future tense. "I'm going to do better, I promise."

Evan's mom folded her arms and stared at Brady for a long time. "Is he telling the truth?" she asked Evan, finally.

"He is," said Evan. "Absolutely."

Evan's statement seemed to change something inside of Ms. Pao. Her hands dropped to her side. "You're just a kid," she said. Her voice shook.

Ms. Pao said something in Chinese. Brady looked at Evan for a translation. Evan shrugged. Ms. Pao made a sound. *Ai ya!* Brady didn't know the words, but he knew the tone. Parental irritation.

"You should know this," said Ms. Pao to Evan. She repeated the sounds, more slowly, and then explained them. "People at birth are basically good. But . . . they become different if they are not properly taught." Then she looked away and blinked. "Come back tomorrow."

"Ma'am?" He was certain he had misheard her.

248

"I need time. Come back tomorrow," she said impatiently. Brady looked at Evan for guidance. Evan looked as puzzled as Brady felt. "I guess you should come back tomorrow," said Evan.

Tomorrow sounded like a beautiful word, even said in an irritated tone. A balm. Room to do better. Room to change.

CHAPTER TWENTY-THREE

EVAN

Evan, Brady, and Max crouched down in the bushes, by the side of Brady's house. The final steps of Evan's plan were finally being carried out.

"I have just confirmed the subject is sleeping," said Brady.

"My dad is holding a staff meeting," said Max. "Emergency calls going out only." He checked his watch. "The meeting will last for another twenty-seven minutes."

"Then let's go," said Evan. "Remember, if we need to scatter, pretend you're looking for Mochi."

"I brought my Frisbee," said Max. "We can act like we're just hanging out." Max and Brady took a few steps into the front yard and began tossing the disc back and forth.

"If I'm the bad one," said Brady. "Why are you guys so good at faking people out?"

"Oh, I know all the schemes from my dad," said Max.

"It's for a good cause," said Evan. Evan got down on his hands and knees, and crawled between the two cars in Brady's driveway so that he was facing the passenger door of Charlie's car. The asphalt warmed his hands and knees. "Are we good?"

"Yup," responded Max and Brady, continuing to throw the Frisbee. "All clear."

The idea had come to Evan a few days before, and once the idea had come into his head, he couldn't let it go, though he had to check with Brady first.

"He's not going to blame you?" Evan had confirmed with Brady, after he told Brady the plan.

"Plenty of people hate that car," said Brady. "I won't be the first person he thinks of. Heck, he's got *friends* who would do something like that."

Now Evan pulled out the white paint pen he'd ordered online with a birthday gift card, and cleaned off a little space on the car door with the hem of his T-shirt. Time to focus. He shook the pen, hearing the mixing balls rattle inside, uncapped the pen, and tried to visualize what he was going to make. He touched the pen to the door. This was it. No going back.

"How long is it going to take you?" asked Max after a few minutes.

"I want it to blend with the other letters," said Evan. "It can't look like a garbage job." The other letters were written in an old English font, with extra swirls and lines. Evan stopped occasionally to consult an alphabet sheet he'd printed out. It was important to pay attention to the height of the letter, the spacing. He had to do it twice—once for each side. On the driver's side, a large rhododendron and a carefully positioned trash can hid Evan from the road.

"Hi, Celeste. Hi, Ella," said Max a little too loudly. Evan froze. He had forgotten that Celeste and Ella went for walks around this time of day, usually followed by watching cooking videos on their phones. Sometimes they even made what they had watched, a practice that Evan heartily approved of.

"Hi, Max. Hi . . . Brady." Celeste was still wary of Brady, though she managed to be polite, if a little remote. "I thought Evan was with you."

"He is," said Brady. "He'll be along in a minute."

Mochi whined and pulled toward the trash can that shielded Evan. "No, Mochi!" scolded Celeste. Mochi's claws scrabbled against the pavement. She bumped the trash can. Evan tucked himself into a tight ball. Mochi could probably smell him. "What have you got in that trash can? Bacon?"

"That would be a crime, throwing away bacon," said Ella dreamily. "I love bacon."

"We should make pasta carbonara!" Celeste said, excited. "I think we have bacon at home, and eggs and pasta." Evan's stomach rumbled loudly in response. Brady coughed over the sound. "Pollen," he croaked.

"We should make our own pasta," said Ella.

"We should! I've heard it's not that hard . . ." The girls' voices slowly faded away.

"All clear," said Brady after a moment. "Also, we're going to your house when we're done, Evan. Sounds like there's going to be food."

Max exhaled loudly. "That was close. I thought Mochi was going to blow your cover."

"Lucky it wasn't Nero," said Evan.

Brady looked up at the house. "Bathroom light just came

on," he said, keeping his voice low. "He usually takes his time in there but you should finish up."

Evan drew a deep breath and willed his hand to stay steady. He finished the last swirl on the driver's side just in time to hear the front door open and bang shut. Evan ducked into a row of bushes against the house, trying not to shake the branches.

"Hey, Max," said Charlie. "Haven't seen you in a while. Still a shrimp, I see." From his place in the bushes, Evan could see Charlie standing in the driveway, watching the two boys throw the Frisbee back and forth.

In his mind, Charlie Griggs was enormous, overshadowing. The one who had shot their house. The angry person at the podium. The owner of the howling screeches in the streets. But looking at him now, Evan realized that Charlie was not that big. He had a soft round belly that hung over the waistband of his jeans. His face was dotted with angry red pimples. He was a person.

Maybe this was what the beginning of justice felt like.

"Hey, Charlie," said Max. "Still unemployed, I see."

"Huh," said Charlie. "Very funny." He got into the car, swinging his keys at the end of a long silver chain. The engine roared to life. The car backed out of the driveway, and then raced down the street, screeching as it banked the corner. The boys ran to the side yard so they could all see what they had accomplished.

Charlie's car now proclaimed NOW MERCY. Instead of rejecting mercy, the car was now hailing it. One letter had changed the message. "Does it look too good?" wondered Max out loud. "Shouldn't it stand out more?"

"It will take him longer to notice," said Brady. "But he will notice."

"I like it," said Evan. "Not bad for a first-time job."

Brady pulled out a small package of gummy bears. "Left over from Halloween," he explained as he doled them out.

"I thought that was Evan's job to bring food," said Max. "And bring food and bring food . . ." Evan punched Max playfully in the shoulder.

"It doesn't matter who brings the food," said Brady. "Just that we have it." Brady tilted his head back and shoved all of his gummy bears into his mouth at once. Evan ate them one by one.

"It is the tradition," said Evan, chewing a pair of pineapple gummy bears vigorously. "Now."

"Now mercy," said Max. And then they started laughing, trying not to spit out candy. Evan hoped people would see the words, notice them. Maybe they would wonder if they had been misreading it all along, puzzled by the combination of the gentle message and the harsh images.

Though why shouldn't mercy show up among skulls and knives and fire? Wasn't mercy just as powerful as intimidation?

Maybe even more.

AUTHOR'S NOTE

This book grew out of a desire to explore two ideas. The first idea was finding out that Chinese men fought in the American Civil War. After years, decades, of having the role of Chinese people in American history limited to the transcontinental railroad, when it is even discussed, my discovery that Chinese men were soldiers in one of our country's most formative wars left me simply agog and wanting more. I wanted to share that moment of uncovering with readers, and then explore how a person might view both the past and the present differently as the result of this additional knowledge.

The second idea came out of my desire to explore themes that arise from working on issues in the criminal legal system. Our current system is rife with shortcomings—one of which is being unable to achieve meaningful reconciliation between two people. My own experience occurred when I was a child; we discovered that someone had shot at our house, twice. Much like Evan's situation, it was the act of a teenage neighbor, driven by racial hatred, though he was actually angry at another group of people; we were just the closest approximation. When my parents went to court, they asked for an apology, which the neighbor refused, and both families ended up moving out of the neighborhood within a year of the incident. I have often wondered what happened to that young man, and if he continued on the path he had started on. I wonder whether a different kind of intervention would have assured that he would make different and better choices in the future.

This story became a question about what it means to be a gentle person in a tough world. At this time, so many people seem to have little capacity for engagement, preferring instead to shout at each other across the Internet, to label, and to shut down important parts of our history. It seems safer to be hard, rather than to contemplate each other's humanity, our mutual foibles, and the fact that we all must live together. The cracks forming in our society are leaving us with few paths to each other.

While writing this book, I came across the Paolo Freire quote, "To speak a true word is to transform the world." Evan's path might not be how everyone could or even should behave, but it reflected his truth and created a connection he would not have had otherwise. It changed his world and the lives of those around him. Evan found a way to stand up for himself, to navigate his own values, and to find strength in his tenderness. For the readers who find themselves in Evan, I hope you do, too.

ACKNOWLEDGMENTS

I am very grateful for the work of Ruthanne Lum McCunn, whose research on Chinese Civil War soldiers inspired and informed this book. Her article, "Chinese in the Civil War: Ten Who Served," shows the astonishing breadth of experiences that brought men to the battlefield. The National Park Service handbook, *Asians and Pacific Islanders and the Civil War*, which included the contributions of many talented writers including McCunn, was also invaluable, as was the website, The Blue, the Gray and the Chinese.

Many, many thanks to Lisa Sandell, who is an endlessly patient and kind editor, and Madelyn Rosenberg, my writing and walking partner par excellence. Shout out to my writing group: Laura, Anna, Ann, Judy, Anamaria, Marty, Carla, Jackie, Susan, Madelyn, and Lenore. Much love and gratitude to my family for their support, much of which involved leaving me alone for swaths of time during a pandemic. I'm ready to come back to earth. XOXO

ABOUT THE AUTHOR

Wendy Wan-Long Shang is the author of *The Great Wall of Lucy Wu*, which was awarded the Asian/Pacific American Award for Children's Literature; *The Way Home Looks Now*, an Amelia Bloomer Project List selection and a CCBC *Choices* List selection; Sydney Taylor Honor Book *This Is Just a Test*, which she cowrote with Madelyn Rosenberg; *Not Your All-American Girl*, a *Tablet* magazine Best Children's Book, also cowritten with Madelyn Rosenberg; and *The Rice in the Pot Goes Round and Round*. Wendy lives with her family in the suburbs of Washington, DC.